"You can't stay here tonight...." Victoria whispered.

"I can," Del said harshly. "And I will."

He took one step toward her. One step was all the room she had. With that simple movement, he robbed her of her safety zone, the shield that kept him at a distance. This close, she could feel his heat, see the stubble on his jaw. The faint, intriguing scent of his body drifted to her.

"You're still angry," he said, his voice softer now.

"Of course I'm still..."

"I'm sorry," he whispered, cupping her chin and forcing her to look him in the eye. And then he kissed her.

She'd known it was coming. She'd known, and yet she hadn't taken her chance to step out of the danger zone and away from this kiss that was going to change *everything*. Her life. His. Her heart...

Dear Reader,

This month we have something really special on tap for you. *The Cinderella Mission*, by Catherine Mann, is the first of three FAMILY SECRETS titles, all of them prequels to our upcoming anthology *Broken Silence* and then a twelve book stand-alone FAMILY SECRETS continuity. These books are cutting edge, combining dark doings, mysterious experiments and overwhelming passion into a mix you won't be able to resist. Next month, the story continues with Linda Castillo's *The Phoenix Encounter*.

Of course, this being Intimate Moments, the excitement doesn't stop there. Award winner Justine Davis offers up another of her REDSTONE, INCORPORATED tales, *One of These Nights*. A scientist who's as handsome as he is brilliant finds himself glad to welcome his sexy bodyguard—and looking forward to exploring just what her job description means. *Wilder Days* (leading to wilder nights?) is the newest from reader favorite Linda Winstead Jones. It will have you turning the pages so fast, you'll lose track of time. Ingrid Weaver begins a new military miniseries, EAGLE SQUADRON, with *Eye of the Beholder*. There will be at least two follow-ups, so keep *your* eyes open so you don't miss them. Evelyn Vaughn, whose miniseries THE CIRCLE was a standout in our former Shadows line, makes her Intimate Moments debut with *Buried Secrets,* a paranormal tale that's as passionate as it is spooky. And Aussie writer Melissa James is back with *Who Do You Trust?* This is a deeply emotional "friends become lovers" reunion romance, one that will captivate you from start to finish.

Enjoy! And come back next month for more of the best and most exciting romance around—right here in Silhouette Intimate Moments.

Leslie J. Wainger
Executive Senior Editor

Please address questions and book requests to:
Silhouette Reader Service
U.S.: 3010 Walden Ave., P.O. Box 1325, Buffalo, NY 14269
Canadian: P.O. Box 609, Fort Erie, Ont. L2A 5X3

Wilder Days
LINDA WINSTEAD JONES

Silhouette®

INTIMATE MOMENTS™

Published by Silhouette Books

America's Publisher of Contemporary Romance

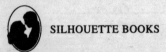 SILHOUETTE BOOKS

ISBN 0-373-27273-1

WILDER DAYS

Copyright © 2003 by Linda Winstead Jones

Printed in U.S.A.

Books by Linda Winstead Jones

Silhouette Intimate Moments

Bridger's Last Stand #924
Every Little Thing #1007
Madigan's Wife #1068
Hot on His Trail #1097
Capturing Cleo #1137
Secret-Agent Sheik #1142
In Bed with Boone #1156
Wilder Days #1203

Silhouette Books

Love Is Murder
"Calling after Midnight"

LINDA WINSTEAD JONES

would rather write than do anything else. Since she cannot cook, gave up ironing many years ago and finds cleaning the house a complete waste of time, she has plenty of time to devote to her obsession for writing. Occasionally she's tried to expand her horizons by taking classes. In the past she's taken instruction on yoga, French (a dismal failure), Chinese cooking, cake decorating (food-related classes are always a good choice, even for someone who can't cook), belly dancing (trust me, this was a long time ago) and, of course, creative writing.

She lives in Huntsville, Alabama, with her husband of more years than she's willing to admit and the youngest of their three sons.

She can be reached via www.eHarlequin.com or her own Web site www.lindawinsteadjones.com.

This book is dedicated to
Leslie Wainger and Mary-Theresa Hussey,
who gave me the chance to tell this story.

Chapter 1

Vic squirmed a little, trying without success to loosen the duct tape that bound her hands behind her back, her ankles to the rear legs of the metal chair, and her bare legs to Del's blue-jeans-encased thighs. She straddled Del, and they were both snugly trussed to the chair and to one another, face-to-face. She glanced down as the man who had dragged her from her home that morning very carefully slid beneath the chair. He cradled something small and deadly looking in his large hands. Vic hadn't thought it possible to be more frightened than she had been since the kidnapping, but the sight of that device made her heart beat a little harder, a little faster.

The second kidnapper, a petite blond woman, handed her partner more duct tape, and he tore off a long strip.

"You said you would let her go when I got here," Del said between clenched teeth.

The blonde looked up at Del and smiled. "I lied."

Del tried, as Vic did, to discreetly loosen the duct tape

that bound him securely to the chair in this second-floor room of a deserted warehouse. Had the sight of that device scared him, too? He didn't seem to be particularly frightened. Mainly, he looked annoyed.

"Whatever happened to professional courtesy?" Del asked, sounding as annoyed as he looked. He kept his eyes on the woman, who continued to kneel by the chair.

Vic shuddered. *Professional courtesy?*

The woman moved aside as her partner slithered from beneath the chair. The fair-haired man rubbed his palms together as he stood. "All done. Let's get out of here."

"You're sure you didn't forget anything?" the woman asked in a low, soothing voice.

"I didn't forget anything." The man sounded slightly offended.

"Good." The blonde's smile returned. "Let's go."

With one last quick wave, they did just that. They left the room, closing the door behind them even though this warehouse somewhere near the interstate had long been abandoned. From what little Vic could see through the uncovered window, they were far from anyone or anything that might be of help. The occasional hum of a large truck passing in the distance was all she could hear. The tops of trees, lush with summer growth, were all she could see through the dirty panes of glass in the single window in this room.

Since they were now alone Vic laid her eyes on Del, and found him staring at her. Eyes dark blue and intense, mouth an unhappy slash, he stared at her as if this was *her* fault.

"That was a bomb," she said softly, wondering if something so simple as a raised voice might set it off.

"Yep."

"We're *sitting* on it."

"Mmm-hmm."

She hadn't seen Del Wilder for sixteen years, until he'd appeared in the doorway of this very room not a half hour ago. Some things about him hadn't changed. He still had long black hair, long legs wrapped in faded denim, a pack of cigarettes in his shirt pocket and a wicked mouth. But he was taller, wider in the shoulders, and occasionally she caught a glimpse of a single glittering diamond earring peeking out from those dark strands of hair. The man was thirty-three years old...no, thirty-four...and he still hadn't managed to completely grow up. Something else to hold against him.

What on earth was he involved in that would lead him, and her, here? Criminal activity, surely. No matter how much she had hated Del Wilder in years past, she'd never thought he might end up some kind of outlaw. Even in her worst moments, she'd thought better of him.

"Well?" she prodded.

"What?"

"Do something!"

He did. He smiled. Had she really once thought that smile irresistibly charming?

"Still painting, I see," he said, nodding his chin.

Vic couldn't do anything about the smudge of paint she knew marred her cheek. Yellow, carried there from a spot of paint on her hands just moments before the doorbell rang. "Yes," she said simply.

Del's eyes traveled from the paint on her cheek to her mouth, to her throat and slowly down the much-too-open V in the worn and paint-stained men's dress shirt Vic wore. At the tip of the V his roving eyes stopped and lingered.

"Do you mind?" Vic asked in her frostiest voice, and the gaze drifted up once again to meet hers.

"How did they get you?" he asked in a low voice. "Please tell me you didn't just open the door and invite them in."

She didn't want to remember, and she certainly didn't want to talk about it. Almost unconsciously, she twitched her nose. She shifted her gaze to the window for a safer view. "I did have the sense to look through the peephole. They were dressed like delivery men," she said.

"*Two* delivery men?" Del asked sharply. "That didn't strike you as unusual?"

Vic shrugged and pursed her mouth. The last thing she needed was to be chastised by Del Wilder! "The box they were pushing on a dolly was quite large. I thought maybe it was very heavy and was too much for one person." She looked Del in the eye again. "The box was for me. They…put me in it."

He nodded, as if he'd already figured that out.

"Who are they?" she asked.

Del took a deep breath and shook his head. "Tripp and Holly Mayron. Drug dealers. Small-time, mostly. Can't figure out what set them off."

Competitors, she imagined, since he'd been so incensed at their lack of professional courtesy. Apparently there was no honor among thieves. Or drug dealers.

Vic's anger faded, just a little. No matter how hard she tried to hate Del Wilder, she couldn't quite get rid of that one little tender spot she still carried for him. "You shouldn't have come here," she said softly.

"I didn't have any choice."

Of course he'd had a choice. Not long after their arrival at this warehouse, the female half of the pair of kidnappers—Holly, she now knew—had dialed a number on the cell phone she'd taken from Vic's entryway table. Until Del had shown up at the door, Vic had thought it was her father they were calling. They'd made Vic say her full name, nothing more, and then Tripp had twisted her arm until she'd cried out. Just once. Holly had told the person on the other end of the phone that he had an hour to get here. If he wasn't here in sixty-one minutes, Victoria Lynn Archard Lowell would be painfully and decisively dead. Directions to this place had followed and less than an hour later Del had arrived.

"You had a choice," she whispered.

After sixteen years, why would Del put his life on the line for her? They'd been together for a day or two less than a month, what seemed like a hundred years ago, thrilling and suffering through an intense teenage romance. It hadn't worked out for them; of course it hadn't. They came from different worlds, and the only thing that had drawn them together had been chemistry. That's all. Some freak biological attraction. She'd told herself that a million times in the past sixteen years.

And here he was.

"Lowell, they said your name was," Del said as he again tried to loosen the duct tape at his back. "Married?"

Her heart hitched. This was not a conversation she wanted to have with Del Wilder, whether they were about to die or not. "Yeah." Not a lie, exactly, since she *had* been married.

"Kids?"

Oh, no. She couldn't handle this. Not now, not ever. "A daughter."

"Just the one?" His eyes no longer bored into hers, but instead were fixed over her shoulder as he concentrated on loosening the tape at his wrists.

Vic nodded. "What about you?" she asked quickly, hoping to change the subject. "Married? Kids?"

Del shook his head. "Nope."

"Why not?"

Again his eyes came to hers. He didn't answer. He was getting frustrated, and his frustration showed more and more on his face.

God, he had a fabulous face. Del had once been almost pretty, but the years had transformed his pretty face into something strikingly masculine and fascinating. She knew that face too well. She knew the distinct lines, the shape of the mouth, the blue of the eyes.

He turned his head toward the window and muttered something. She couldn't decipher it all. There were a few obscenities, and something about shock. Did he think she was going to panic and go into shock? Did she think he would? No, he looked much too calm for that concern.

"I couldn't see the timer on the…the bomb," Vic said in a low voice. "Did you?"

Del nodded, once.

"How much time do we have?"

He hesitated. "We'll be okay."

She didn't think so. She didn't think they were going to be at all *okay.*

She had once loved Del Wilder so deeply and intensely that he had been her entire world. The love hadn't lasted nearly as long as the anger, the disappointment, the heartbreak. Vic didn't let herself expect anything from the people in her life, not anymore. She always ended up disappointed, but these days no one broke her heart. Del had been an important part of her life, long ago, but she didn't owe him anything.

Or did she? If they were going to die here, did he deserve to know that he had a daughter?

Vic had always looked like an angel: flowing wavy hair caught somewhere between brown and gold, cat's eyes of green and gold, lush lips just made for smiling and kissing. She wasn't a girl anymore, she was a woman, nicely filled out and without the little bit of baby fat that had made her cheeks round and pink, years ago. She was leaner in the face today, shapelier everywhere else.

But of course Vic was not an angel and never had been. She was a mere mortal, with flaws all her own. Del took some comfort from the fact that she was currently sweating like a pig.

Where was Shock? He should have been here by now. Something had happened, something had delayed the planned rescue. They were going to have to get out of here themselves.

"Know what I remember about you?" he asked, smiling crookedly at Vic.

"What?" she asked, as if she really didn't want to know. Smart girl.

"Your flexibility."

She looked offended. "*That's* what you remember?"

"You could twist your legs, turn your body, bend…"

"All right," she snapped. "I get the picture. Know what I remember about you? I remember that you were nothing but trouble. I remember that you were the most stubborn, arrogant, possessive, egotistical…"

"Vic, this isn't helping matters any."

"And your observations have some deeper meaning?"

Again, he smiled. "There's a knife in my right boot."

Her anger faded. "There is?"

"I can't reach it, but maybe you can."

She nodded, shook her hair back and began to tilt to the side, her face taut with determination.

"Vic, honey," Del said calmly. "My other right boot."

She straightened quickly, gave him a sharp glance that told him it was somehow his fault she had moved to her right and not his, and began again.

Vic was the woman he had spent the past sixteen years trying to forget. Some days he actually succeeded. But when he'd heard her name being whispered over the phone, his heart had just about stopped. Maybe because she was his first. First love, first lover, first real experience with pain. It was perfectly natural that he sometimes remembered her fondly.

And surely it was also perfectly natural that as she moved to the side and her shirt shifted, he was distracted by the new expanse of breast that was exposed. A pale, soft-looking swell of flesh that momentarily took his mind off of everything else.

Del did his best to shake off the distraction. Couldn't the woman wear a bra? If he didn't know better, he'd think Vic was doing this to him on purpose.

Vic's shorts were short, the legs that were wrapped around him were smooth and strong. He hated that his hands were tied. More than anything, he wanted to run his palm up her leg, slow and easy.

Her fingers skimmed down his calf as she reached blindly for the sheath and the knife inside his boot.

What was wrong with him? He hadn't seen her for sixteen years, and their last parting had been ugly, to say the least. She was married, a mother, the woman who had once been the girl who had broken his heart. In the years since he'd left her behind, he'd cursed her, longed for her and almost forgotten her.

And right now he *wanted* her. Nothing else mattered enough to get in the way of that.

"Almost there," she whispered, licking her lips as she stretched and moved just a little bit more. She smiled when she finally found and grabbed the handle of the knife. "Got it." A grin that didn't last long flitted across her face. It was the first time he'd seen her smile since he'd walked into this room. Of course, she hadn't had much to smile about today.

Vic straightened cautiously, the knife behind her back.

"If you can just knick the edge of the tape at your wrists," Del said calmly, "you should be able to rip it apart. Once your hands are loose, we're home free."

She nodded and began, her face once again rigid with concentration. Those cat's eyes were fixed on the center of his forehead as she worked.

"I wish it wasn't so hot in here," she said softly. "My palms are slick with sweat."

"It's okay, baby. You're doing great."

Her eyes met his, briefly, and then she stared at his forehead again as she continued her efforts. "So close," she whispered beneath her breath. "I just can't quite…"

She cursed, flinched, and the knife clattered to the floor. Her eyes met his again, and he saw something new. Panic.

"I'm sorry," she whispered. "I tried to catch it, I did, but it just slipped right through my fingers."

"Did you cut yourself?"

She nodded.

"How bad?"

"Not too bad, I think. It just stings a little."

He kept his knife sharp. If the blade had brushed past her fingers, the cuts might be deep.

Cuts on Vic's fingers were the least of their problems, and still that knowledge bothered Del more than it should. If she wasn't here, he'd knock the chair to its side and try to free himself from that position, but he couldn't take the chance. What he'd seen on the side of the explosive device that had been taped to the bottom of the chair looked to be a tilt detonator. If the chair tipped over, the bomb would go off. He didn't mind taking chances with his own life. He wouldn't— couldn't—take that risk with Vic's.

"I'm sorry," she said again, softer this time.

"It's okay," he said, trying to ease her distress with a smile.

"You keep saying that," she said, growing visibly frustrated. Her cheeks flushed, her chest rose and fell with deeper, faster breaths. "Nothing is okay!"

While he thought about what came next, he had to calm her down. He had to get her talking about something else, *anything* else. "A daughter, huh?"

Her eyes widened, her spine straightened. "Yes."

"What's she like?" Mothers liked talking about their kids, right? He might have asked about the husband, but in truth he didn't want to know about Vic's marriage. He didn't want to hear her talk about the man who shared her bed.

Vic took a deep breath. "Noelle," she said. "Her name is Noelle."

Del nodded. "Nice name. How old is she?"

Vic hesitated. This wasn't working. Talking about her daughter was not calming Vic in any way. "Fourteen," she finally whispered.

"Tough age," Del said, trying to carry the conversation along. "Is she as pretty as you were at fourteen?" he teased.

"Prettier."

"Not possible."

Vic's eyes latched on to his. She took a deep breath, and something in her changed, slowly and subtly. "Noelle is much more beautiful than I ever was. She's smart, too, and has a real talent for drawing." Her lips parted and softened. "She hates that, that she inherited a talent from me."

"She'd rather be like her father?"

Vic shook her head. "No. I sometimes think Noelle wishes she'd sprung from a pod, fully grown and beholden to no one."

"Sounds like fourteen to me," Del said, his voice low. His smile faded. "Was she home this morning?"

Vic shook her head. "No, thank God. She's in Gulf Shores with a friend's family. They went on vacation and Michelle refused to go without her best friend." Finally, she smiled again. "You should see her," she whispered. "She's so...so much like..." She stopped, her throat worked gently, and she shook her head. "Del..."

In the distance, he heard a muted noise. With a whispering breath, he shushed Vic. "Hear that?"

"Hear what?"

"A car." He strained as he listened hard. "A car door."

She began to tremble. "Do you think they came back?"

Del shook his head. "Nope. I think it's the cavalry. Can you scream, baby?"

Vic shook her head, and Del shouted. "Up here!" Vic jumped, as if her entire body had been shocked. She didn't scream. "Hurry!" Del shouted again when he heard footsteps pounding on the stairs.

"If it is the cavalry," Vic whispered, "are they too late? How much time do we have?"

Del smiled. "Enough, I think."

"You *think?*" Vic asked.

The door to the room burst open, and Vic almost fainted. Her vision blurred and her head swam. This couldn't possibly be the cavalry. The man who stood in the doorway was small, very thin. His hair was as long as Del's, and the fine strands were a dirty dark blond instead of Del's thick black. His eyes were…buggy, his face was pale. He held a gun in one hand and a knife in the other and he was poised to do battle.

"It's about time," Del snapped. "Get us out of here."

The little man holstered his gun. "Sorry I'm late," he said as he came toward them with the knife grasped in his hand. "I got lost. Took the wrong exit." He glared accusingly at Del. "Man, your one looked like a seven. Anyway, I turned around and headed back this way…."

"Shock," Del snapped, "I hate to interrupt, but there's a bomb taped to the underside of the chair. How about take a peek and see how much time we have left."

The man Del called Shock complied, dropping down and sticking his head beneath the chair. The single word that came out of his mouth did nothing to soothe Vic's nerves.

"I hate bombs," he said as he returned to an upright position and began to decisively and expertly cut away the duct tape that bound Vic and Del together and to the chair. "*Hate* 'em."

"Tilt detonator?" Del asked.

"Yup," Shock said as he continued to cut.

"How's our time?"

"Shorter than I'd like."

As Shock moved behind Vic, he whistled through his teeth. "You're bleeding," he said without slowing his chore.

"It's not too bad," Vic said, her voice not rising as much as she'd intended.

Shock just made a noise, something between a groan and a hum.

When she was free, Vic thought about standing. And couldn't. Her legs shook. Her hands trembled. She glanced down at the gashes on her fingers as Shock cut the last of Del's bonds away. Blood dripped down her palm, across her wrist.

When Del was free, he put his arms around her, assisted her to her feet and led her from the room. Quickly. Shock was right behind, doing his best to hurry them along. Del, one arm securely around Vic's waist, pulled her so quickly her feet barely touched the ground as they flew down the stairs.

She wasn't exactly thinking rationally. Halfway down the stairs, she came up short. "My cell phone is still up there."

"Screw the cell phone," Del grumbled as he dragged Vic off her feet and down the rest of the stairs.

They ran through the double front doors, into the bright summer sunshine. Vic apparently wasn't running fast enough to suit Del; he dragged her along. A moment after they left the building, Shock appeared at her other side.

"Let's go," he said as he added his arm around her waist.

The two men pulled her along, her feet off the ground, her heart caught in her throat. They had reached the

parking lot and were running hard toward the two cars
at the far end when the explosion rocked the building
behind them. The noise was deafening, the blast of heat
unnatural even on this summer day. Shattering glass was
loud, a strangely pretty, dangerous sound. Shards landed
in the parking lot, just behind them. As she heard the
glass land on the asphalt, Vic was glad Del and Shock
had grabbed her up and hurried her along. They didn't
look back, not until they reached the cars.

Vic's heart sank as she studied those cars, a black
Jaguar and an electric-blue Dodge Viper. Those two ve-
hicles together surely cost more than her house. Del
Wilder, a *drug dealer*. She couldn't believe it. "At least
they didn't take your Jag," Shock said.

Del responded without emotion. "Even Tripp and
Holly are too smart for that. They want to disappear and
a Jag is definitely not a ride that makes you invisible."

Vic listened, but her mind was elsewhere. She had
almost told Del about Noelle, she had almost confessed
to him that they had a child together. That could never
happen. Never. If someone would try to get to Del
through her, what would they do if they knew he had a
daughter?

They watched the building burn.

"Did they get your Glock?" Shock asked.

"Yep," Del answered.

Shock mumbled an obscenity, then turned to Vic and
smiled, presenting a grin that was all teeth and gums.
"Name's Albert Shockley, ma'am," he said. "But you
can call me Shock. A name should suit a person, you
know? I don't know what my mother was thinking when
she named me Albert." He waited a moment. "And you
are?"

"Vic," she said, the name barely passing through her lips.

Shock's smile faded a little, and he turned a suspicious glance to Del, who continued to watch the spreading fire.

"Vic," Shock repeated. "Now, that's just not right. Vic is a name for a fat, smelly guy, not a pretty lady. Gotta be short for something."

"Victoria," she whispered.

Del tore his attention away from the burning warehouse and took her hand in his, studying the cuts on her fingers. Again, he cursed.

"It'll be okay," she said, trying to draw her hand from his tight grasp.

Del held fast. There was no withdrawing her hand from his, not unless he wanted her to. "Baby," he growled, "nothing is okay."

Chapter 2

Vic hadn't looked him in the eye since they'd left the warehouse parking lot, and the only words she'd spoken had been lifeless directions to her South Huntsville home. He'd bandaged her hand quickly, using the first-aid kit he always had in the trunk, while Shock had checked the Jag inside and out for nasty explosive devices. Shock had found nothing, and they'd gotten out of there while the fire raged. They were gone long before the volunteer fire department could arrive.

Del steered the Jag in and out of shaded portions of the street, driving slowly since there were kids everywhere. They played ball, rode bikes, attempted tricks on skateboards and in-line skates. It was a nice neighborhood. The homes were nothing like the antebellum house in Old Town where Vic had grown up, but nice just the same.

"Here," she said, pointing to an empty driveway. Del turned sharply and came to an abrupt stop before a midsize, middle-class Colonial home. Two stories, neatly landscaped, nothing special that might reach out and grab a person. It was just…a house.

"Thanks," Vic said as she opened the passenger door and stepped out of the car. Still, she didn't look directly at him.

Del cursed beneath his breath. She'd survived the crisis and now she was falling apart. Women did that, or so he'd been told.

He left the car and headed for Vic's slow-moving form, tempted to put his arm around her as he had when they'd run from the warehouse. She looked like she needed the support, but he didn't touch her. He stayed close, though, just in case.

She stepped onto the porch and reached out to touch the doorknob. The door easily swung open. Finally, she looked up at him. "They didn't lock the door." From the tone of her voice, it was clear she found this the most egregious of the Mayrons' sins.

"Should anyone be here?"

Vic shook her head.

Del drew the Colt pistol Shock had pressed upon him before they left the warehouse, taking care that the weapon was not visible to anyone passing on the street. "Stay here," he said softly as he left Vic waiting on the front porch.

His search of the house was quick, efficient and productive in an unexpected way. No one was waiting for Vic's return. Tripp and Holly, who were not the most brilliant of the criminals he'd run across in his career, had been sloppily confident that there was nothing wrong with their plan. They actually thought that Del would take their warning that they would know if he told anyone where he was going seriously.

After talking to Holly and hearing Vic say her name and then cry out, Del had written a quick note and slipped it to Shock quietly, in case the caller had been telling the truth and he was being watched. He'd suspected all along that threat was false; he knew the other agents in the office too well to suspect that they'd be involved in anything like this. But he couldn't take the chance that he was right about them all. Not with Vic's life at stake.

The quick check of her neat home revealed something interesting. The men's shirt she wore was the only piece of men's clothing in the house. There was no electric razor in the bathroom, no men's shoes in the closet…nothing. This was a woman's house, pure and simple, put together with an easy blending of soft colors and comfortable furniture. The only exception was the daughter's bedroom, which was decorated in purple and black and adorned with slick posters of bands Del had never heard of. From the looks of the guys in the posters, they weren't exactly into easy listening.

"All clear," he said, placing the pistol at his spine as he opened the front door and reached out a hand to assist Vic over the threshold.

She nodded her head, obviously relieved, and stepped inside, releasing his hand as she walked through the foyer. Unconsciously, he was sure, her fingertips trailed across the palm of his hand. "Thanks. Should I…do anything? Call the police?" She turned slowly and tilted her head back, looking him squarely and bravely in the eye. "I won't," she said. "Not if you don't want me to."

He knew how this looked, what she was thinking. With a few words he could set her straight. He said nothing, telling himself it no longer mattered what Vic thought.

"I'll handle it," he said, his voice low.

She just nodded. "Thanks for the ride." It was a neat, almost polite dismissal.

"Coffee," Del said, brushing past her. "And I need to use your phone."

"There's a café on the corner and they have great coffee," she said quickly. "And they have a phone, too. I think," she added in a softer voice.

Del turned before he reached the short hallway that led to the kitchen. "Trying to get rid of me?"

Vic nodded.

"I can't leave you here alone." Del leaned his shoulder against the wall and crossed his arms over his chest, relaxing outside even as tension coiled inside him. Vic had been less than forthcoming. "I thought maybe I'd wait around until your husband gets home. Is he at work? You can give him a call and…"

"That's not necessary," she said, her voice low and quick, her eyes darting away from him. At least she had the good manners to look a little guilty as she lied.

"What's his name?" Del asked.

"Preston," Vic whispered. "Preston Lowell."

"And when will he be home?" How many chances was he going to give her to tell him the truth?

Her face went pale, once again. Her usually luscious lips thinned and tightened. "We're divorced," she finally admitted. "He lives in North Carolina."

Del smiled. "You forgot to mention that earlier." He turned and headed for the kitchen. "Pack a bag," he said as he walked away. "We're getting out of here."

He heard Vic's footsteps behind him, the pad of her tennis shoes soft on the tile floor. "No. That's not necessary. The bomb blew up, surely those two will think we're dead. Right?'' That last word was tinged with hope.

"For a couple of days," Del answered. "Eventually they'll wonder why there's no mention of the bodies on the news, and they'll do a little digging. Won't take them long to find out the building was empty when it blew. You're not safe here."

He expected Vic to argue, but his declaration was met with dead silence.

He found the coffee and filters in the most logical place—in the cabinet above the coffeemaker. While Vic watched, he measured out the grounds and got the brew going. When he turned around, he found Vic staring at him so hard he could feel it.

"Why me?" she asked. "I haven't seen you for sixteen years. It doesn't make sense that they would kidnap *me* to get to you."

He'd had the same thought. Why her? True, the assignment to Birmingham, Alabama, put them in the same geographical area, but still...there had been other women in his life. Women who'd lasted more than a month. But then, Vic hadn't been a woman sixteen years ago, she'd been a little girl playing with womanly things.

"I don't know," he admitted. "But I'm going to find out."

She nodded her head and looked away from him.

"How's the hand?"

She wiggled the tightly bandaged fingers. "Fine."

An awkward silence filled the air of Vic's homey, bright kitchen. The coffeemaker gurgled, and outside a bird chirped. The light that broke through the wide window at the breakfast nook bathed Vic in a way that made her look golden, more beautiful than she really was, surely. Del tried to tell himself that he no longer cared for her, that she didn't grab him somewhere deep inside and hold on.

"They're going to come back, aren't they?" Her voice was breathless with fear.

"I don't know," he admitted. "I don't think so. And they won't be back tonight, that's certain. They want to be far, far away when you come up missing or dead. If they decided to come back and swipe your TV or rifle through your jewelry box like common thieves, someone might see them in the area. It's not a chance they'll take. You need to get out of here, though, because when they find out you're not dead they'll be back. Like I said, we have a little time."

She nodded. "Noelle's not supposed to be back for four days."

"We don't have that much time. Should we go to Gulf Shores and pick her up?"

Vic's eyes were condemning, sharp and no longer afraid. "We? No. I'll go get her myself."

Del shook his head. "I can't let you do that." Dammit, there was no way he'd leave Vic to handle this on her own. He couldn't.

"*Let* me?" Vic snapped.

Her defiance was almost amusing. Almost. "You have no idea what you're up against. I can't just *let* you run out of here on your own."

"What are you going to do, tag along?"

Del sighed, not at all happy with this turn of events. "Yeah."

Del refused to leave, even when Vic reached the end of her rope and threatened to call the police. He said one night in the house would be all right. The television news had covered the explosion of the abandoned warehouse off of I-65, and while they hadn't reported anything about discovering bodies inside, there hadn't been much information at all. The fire had still been too hot for investigators to explore the building.

Maybe right now the kidnappers thought she and Del were dead. That incorrect assumption would not last long.

So come tomorrow morning, she and Del were headed for Gulf Shores to collect Noelle. Then what? Oh, it was not a good idea for those two to be together, not even for a short time. Noelle had Del's black hair, his blue eyes, his way of finding and embracing trouble. Would he take one look at her and *know?*

Del finished making his phone calls in the kitchen and walked into the living room where Vic was curled up on the couch. She couldn't help herself…she was taken aback by how beautiful he was, how unexpectedly tempting. Talk about trouble! Del Wilder was a criminal who had come back into her life with a bang. Literally. He couldn't stay, and she couldn't let herself be tempted by what she couldn't have.

"I'll hire someone to go with me," she said, not sounding as confident as she wanted to. "A private investigator, maybe, someone who specializes in personal protection."

"Still trying to get rid of me?"

"Yes."

He ignored her, smiled and walked to the mantel where a collection of photographs were carefully placed. Vic's heart almost stopped when he reached out and grabbed an eight-by-ten of Noelle at the age of nine. She'd been taking dance lessons then, and was wearing a ladybug outfit, complete with wings and antennae.

Vic's heart thudded too hard. What if he looked at Noelle and saw the truth?

"Pretty girl," he said, smiling as he returned the framed photo to its place.

"Yes, she is."

"So," Del said, turning to face her. "What happened with Presley?"

"Preston," she said tersely. "And what happened to my marriage is none of your business."

"Just curious. Trying to kill a little time." He shoved his hands in his pocket, the move making him look like a large, tense, restless boy. "Shock will come by in the morning and drop off a bag. I'd like to get out of here pretty early. By ten, anyway."

"Del…"

"And don't tell me I'm not going with you," he interrupted. "You need me, Vic."

Those were the last words she wanted to hear! "I do *not* need you."

She didn't need anyone to look out for her or Noelle. The only men who had ever tried to shelter and protect her had ended up betraying her, in one way or another. Her father; Preston. Even Del. These days Vic looked out for herself and her daughter. She didn't need a man to play the hero.

"At least let me see you settled somewhere safe," Del said, obviously trying to placate her. "I know of a few good places to hide."

"I'm sure you do."

Del grinned at her blatant insult. "You got tough while I was gone."

He couldn't possibly know what a nerve he'd touched on. "I didn't have any choice."

* * *

Shock was right on time, for a change, and he came bearing everything Del had asked for. Clothes, ammo, an extra pistol. And a file on Vic and her ex-husband.

Del enjoyed his morning ritual, coffee and a cigarette, and flipped through the file. There wasn't much.

"Any luck finding Tripp and Holly?"

Shock shook his head. "No, man, they're staying clear of their regular haunts. They'll turn up sooner or later. They always do."

Up until now, the Mayrons had been a minor annoyance, two pesky flies in the ointment. They hadn't been this determined, violent or organized before. Besides, Tripp Mayron was a major screwup.

"And the other?"

"Most of the good stuff is up here," Shock said, tapping a fingertip against his temple. "I made a few phone calls last night and dug up the real dirt."

Del looked down at a photo of Vic, an impersonal and unflattering driver's license picture. And still, she looked good. "Let's hear it."

"Six years ago Preston Lowell, who works for Vic's old man, was caught with his pants down. Literally. Not a pretty sight, from what I hear. The guy's apparently got a really tiny little…"

"Shock," Del growled in warning.

"Old man Archard, his secretary and a new client walked into Preston's office after hours to get some papers or something, and found naughty Lowell and his new secretary…dictating, right there on the desk." Shock waggled his eyebrows. "Vic kicked him out and he got transferred to the Raleigh office, a demotion from what I hear. Vic had already been selling some paintings, but once she was on her own she really threw herself

into the business. Now she releases several prints a year
and makes a decent living doing it.''

Del stared at the grainy photograph. He wasn't sorry
that Vic was currently unattached, but he was incensed
that any man would treat her that way. She deserved
better.

''By the way, this is *the* Vic, right?'' Shock's long,
thin fingers danced over his heart.

''Shut up, Albert,'' Del muttered.

Shock clapped a hand over his heart. ''Man, I do you
a favor and you call me Albert. What's gotten into
you?''

Del lifted his eyes slowly. ''Anything else?''

''Only that no one at Archard Enterprises likes Preston much, and that he'd been fooling around for years.
Everybody knew, probably even Vic. Once the old man
caught him, though, that was his ass.''

''But he was demoted, not fired?'' Del shook his head.
''The old man should have kicked his butt and then run
him out of town on a rail, but instead he transfers him
to Raleigh?''

Shock just grunted, in a familiar kind of ac-
knowledgment.

Del took a long drag on his cigarette. ''Okay, the old
man is screwed up. I already knew that. But if Lowell
had been fooling around for years…why would Vic put
up with that?''

''Why don't you just ask me?''

He and Shock both turned their heads toward the
kitchen doorway to find an irate Vic standing there, her
hair curling wildly, her thick white robe cinched tight.
She stepped toward Del and he tried to close the file.
Too late. She saw her own picture.

''Vic, baby…'' he began.

"Don't you *Vic, baby* me," she snapped, reaching out and taking the cigarette from his fingers, tossing it into his coffee cup. "And don't smoke in my house!"

Del glanced down at what was left of his cigarette floating in what was left of his coffee. What a waste. "Like it or not, you're as much a part of this as I am."

"Yeah, right." She crossed her arms over her chest. There was fire in her eyes, color in her cheeks and pink nail polish on her toes. What a woman. "I'm an artist. No matter how unhappy someone might be with a painting I do, they don't try to blow me up!"

"We have to cover every possibility."

"No, we don't," she said calmly. "Get out of my house before I call the police." With that, she turned her back on him.

"Nothing's changed, Vic," he called after her. "As soon as you're dressed, we'll go pick up the kid and find a safe place for you both."

"No, thank you."

"Fine, then," he said, growing angry at her stubbornness. "Call the police. Someone there will surely talk. It'll hit the newspapers, maybe even the noon news. And the next thing you know Tripp and Holly will know we didn't go up with the warehouse and they'll be back."

She spun on him. "It'll be worth it to see you in jail."

"Jail?" Shock said. "Man, what did you do?"

Del kept his eyes on Vic. "Nothing. Vic just has some mistaken ideas about what my life has been like. Isn't that right, baby?"

She turned red. "It doesn't exactly take a genius to figure it out."

He reached into his back pocket, drew out his ID and flipped it open to display the badge. "DEA," he said. "Did you figure that one out?"

She stared at the badge from a distance. "Drug Enforcement Administration," she said softly, obviously surprised. Her brow wrinkled, her lips thinned. "Why didn't you tell me this yesterday?"

He shrugged. "I work undercover. The idea is not to tell everyone in the world what I do."

She looked hurt, as if it pained her to be clumped in with everyone else in the world. Did she think she still meant something to him, that she was special? No, too many years had passed for that.

"Del is the best," Shock said, breaking an uncomfortable silence. "We've been partners for five years," he added. "There was this one time—"

"Not now," Del interrupted.

"Sure, man."

Del stared at an angry Vic. "Pack your bag and let's get out of here."

"I don't..."

"What are you going to do the next time the doorbell rings, Vic? Hide? Take a chance and open the door on God knows what? Tripp and Holly might hire out the dirty work, since you've seen their faces. Anyone who comes to your door could be the bad guy, and next time they might decide to take your daughter, too."

Her face went white.

"You saw them, you can testify against them, and they won't forget that. We're leaving in thirty minutes," he added. "Whether you're ready or not, whether you want to or not." His own anger rose. "If I have to toss you over my shoulder and carry you out of here, I will. Don't doubt it, Vic."

She gave him one last, less-than-warm look before turning her back on him. "I don't doubt it at all."

*   *   *

They'd been riding in silence for more than an hour, Del concentrating on the road, Vic staring out the passenger window. The tension was so thick you could cut it with a knife. She couldn't stand another five hours of this.

"We're going to have to call a truce," she said calmly.

"What kind of truce?"

Del was no happier with her than she was with him. She had no need to worry that he might complicate matters where Noelle was concerned. As soon as he could get rid of them both with a clear conscience, he would.

"We're both going to have to compromise."

"I'm already compromising," he muttered. "I'm driving a freakin' minivan."

Vic smiled. "We couldn't get everything in your Jaguar and have room for Noelle in that tiny excuse for a back seat."

"I know."

"I'm sure your car will be safe in my garage."

He just mumbled.

"So," she continued. "Truce?"

"Sure."

Del glanced at her and she smiled as if it didn't hurt. There had been days when she prayed to be able to forget him, but how could she? Noelle was so much like him that sometimes it frightened her. The similarities went beyond coloring and the shape of their mouths. Noelle had Del's restless spirit, his pride and his ingrained defiance.

"So," she said, trying for a light conversational tone. "How have you been?"

He laughed, and the sound was unexpectedly heartwarming. Del had never laughed much, but when he did the laughter came from his heart and soul. "Fine. And you?"

"Fine." Memories she didn't want came rushing back. "Did you ever learn to dance?"

"Yep."

"Good," she whispered.

"Did you ever learn to swim?"

"No." She found she didn't want to know how many women had been in Del's life, so she didn't even bother to ask if he'd ever been married. She suspected not. Del had never been one for settling down, and since the kidnappers who were after him had needed bait, it had been her they'd kidnapped. After all these years...

"I tried to teach you," he said, shaking his head. "But you wouldn't..." He stopped suddenly. Did he remember, too?

It had been too early in the year to swim, the water too cold, and she had held on to Del with everything she had while the water lapped around them, the lights of the pool they'd sneaked into making the night eerie and romantic. Romantic to a silly seventeen-year-old girl, anyway. God, she had loved holding on to him.

"Once we have Noelle with us, where are we going?" she asked, anxious to change the subject. Being in close quarters with Del was bad enough. Bringing back old memories that would do neither of them any good only made matters worse.

Del stared at her, but he didn't answer for a few long minutes. Finally he said, "Don't worry. I have everything taken care of."

Not *everything,* she imagined. There were too many details Del didn't know, too many things he couldn't possibly be prepared for.

How could she prepare him for Noelle? Noelle, who

was so much like him, who rebelled at every turn…who would not be happy to see them.

Much as he'd like to think otherwise, Del did *not* have everything under control.

Chapter 3

"Who the hell are you?"

Del was a little taken aback. *This* was Vic's daughter? The teenage girl stood in the main room of a very nice condo on the beach, shooting daggers at him with her eyes. Vic's pride and joy was dressed entirely in black, from her clunky tennis shoes to the baggy shorts to the oversize T-shirt. There were, at quick count, six earrings in one ear. Only one in the other. And her *head*...

"Noelle Eve Lowell," Vic said, sounding horrified. "What have you done to your hair?"

The teenager took audacious eyes off of Del and laid them on her mother. "It rained yesterday. We didn't have anything to do." She touched a hand to her hair, which was a very unnatural shade of red and cut too short...on one side. On the other side, soft red strands brushed softly against one cheek.

"It rained," Vic said, "and you just happened to have hair dye with you? And a pair of scissors, too, I see?"

"We brought them with us just in case." Noelle shuffled one foot. "Michelle's hair turned pink and I think I cut it too short on one side. Her mom is really *not* happy." Her expression hardened. "Why are you here, Mother, and who is the thug?"

Thug?

"Please tell me you're not going through a midlife crisis and actually *sleeping* with this guy."

"Noelle!"

"And if you are, why did you feel the need to drive all the way down here to, what…introduce us? I really don't need to be dragged into your midlife crisis, Mother."

The three of them were alone in the classy, nicely furnished condo. The Severns, Noelle's friend's family, were down at the beach. Just as well.

"We're taking a little vacation," Del said calmly.

Noelle glared at him. "I'm already on vacation, moron. And I still don't know who you are."

He'd dealt with tough customers before, many of them tougher than Vic's daughter. Maybe. "Del Wilder," he said, stepping forward and offering his hand. "Your mother and I are old friends."

Behind him, Vic continued to mutter about her daughter's hair.

"Old friends. How nice." Instead of extending her hand to shake Del's, Noelle placed hands on hips and struck a defiant pose. "Why on earth do you want me along on your little vacation? I'm sure to cramp your style."

Vic had decided that she didn't want Noelle to know what had happened. Not yet, anyway. Del had to agree. It was sure to be traumatic for a fourteen-year-old to know that someone had just tried to blow up her mother.

"Family vacation," Del grumbled.

"You're not family."

He ignored her. "Fishing, picnics, a cabin by the lake." He hadn't told Vic where they were going, but she'd know soon enough. The cabin he'd rented was close enough to Birmingham that he could make a run to the office, if he had to, far enough away from town that they wouldn't have to worry about being spotted by anyone passing by. No one but Shock knew the location of the hideaway.

"I *hate* fishing."

Del had a feeling he and Noelle could stand here all day and never agree on anything. If he told her the sky was blue, she'd come up with some kind of argument. He'd rather face the business end of a gun than deal with an obviously mixed-up fourteen-year-old.

Vic stepped forward, passing close to Del as she approached her daughter. "Pack your things and let's go," she said.

Noelle opened her mouth to argue, but Vic didn't give her a chance.

"Now."

Noelle sighed, but she turned around and disappeared into a bedroom to do as her mother asked.

Del crept up behind Vic and laid a hand on her shoulder. "She hates me."

"She'll get over it."

He tried to think of something positive to say. The words stuck in his throat, until he finally said, "She's a pretty girl."

"Yes," Vic said softly. "She is." Beneath his hand, he felt Vic relax. "Don't take anything she says too seriously. The past couple of years have been tough."

Del's thumb rocked against Vic's shoulder, an easily offered comfort she didn't brush away. "The divorce?"

Vic nodded. "At first, she didn't really understand. I think she spent years waiting…waiting for Preston to come home. When she finally realized that he wasn't coming home, she got angry. She's still angry, but she'll be okay." Vic took a deep, stilling breath. "The tough-girl image is an act, mostly."

Del nodded. "I understand." Okay, it was a lie. He *didn't* understand. But since he wouldn't be around long, he didn't need to, right?

He didn't like the uncertainty that washed through him. What if he *was* around for a while? What if even after the Mayrons were caught and Vic was safe, he continued to see her?

Like she'd let him. Vic had made it clear that truce or no truce, he was not welcome in her life.

The spot Del had chosen as their hideout didn't look like much, but Vic approached the cabin with the hope that the inside would be better.

It wasn't.

"Oh, my God," Noelle said as she stepped from the sagging front porch into the main room of the sprawling cabin. "This is a joke, right? We're not actually going to *sleep* here."

"Haven't you ever heard of roughing it, kid?" Del asked with a wide smile on his face.

"This was all your idea, wasn't it, Wilder?" Noelle asked, casting a narrow-eyed glance over her shoulder.

Del's grin remained in place.

Noelle began to explore, very quickly discovering that there was no phone and no air-conditioning. She expressed overly exuberant delight upon finding indoor plumbing.

While Noelle disappeared down the hallway to choose the bedroom that would be her own, Vic faced Del.

"I'm sure we'll be okay here," she said, steeling herself to send Del away. "Thanks. When all's clear, I guess you'll let me know. Right?" Her heart caught in her throat as she looked up at him; her mouth went dry. He had to get out of here. What if one morning he looked at Noelle and just *knew?* Then what?

She didn't like the way he looked at her, his smile fading, his eyes going dark. "Who said I was going anywhere?"

"You can't…"

"I can," he interrupted. "And I will."

He took one step toward her. One step was all the room she had. With that simple move he robbed her of her safety zone, her personal space, the shield that kept him at a distance. This close she could feel his heat, see the stubble on his jaw. The faint, intriguing scent of his body drifted to her.

"You're still angry," he said softly.

"Of course I'm still…"

"I'm sorry," he whispered, cupping her chin and forcing her to look him in the eye. "I should have told you what I do as soon as I had the chance. It's just that when I realized what you thought, it hurt a little."

"What else was I supposed to think?"

He nodded, once. "Fair enough."

"You…you investigated me," she said in an accusatory tone of voice.

"Yes, I did."

"Why?"

Del hesitated. "I can't assume anything, Vic. I need

to find out why they went after you. There are other ways to get to me. I can't figure out how they connected us. It's been such a long time." He moved a little bit closer.

"So investigating me was just...part of the job."

"No." His head dipped. "I wanted to know."

"You wanted to know what?"

"Everything." With every heartbeat he moved closer.

Vic licked her lips. "There's not much to know. My life is...pretty dull. At least..."

Del kissed her. She'd known it was coming, had passed and ignored her chance to step out of the danger zone and away from this kiss that was going to complicate everything. Her life. His. Her heart.

She loved the way Del kissed, his lips gentle and firm, his body molding to hers and his arms wrapping around her. He gave everything he had to this kiss, the way he had always given everything of himself to whatever he did. The movement of his mouth over hers rocked her to her core, made her forget everything else.

His tongue swept over her bottom lip, and she couldn't contain the catch in her throat that gave away her response. One caressing hand was in her hair, the other stayed firmly at her spine. Every now and then his fingers rocked, comforting and much too arousing.

There was comfort in a kiss. She had forgotten that. She had also forgotten what it was like to be swept away by physical sensation. To feel as if she were melting, as if her knees might buckle at any moment. Her lips parted more widely, as unconsciously she invited more. And more.

"This," a cold voice called from too nearby, "is totally disgusting."

The kiss ended abruptly and Del backed up a step just

as Vic did. To his credit, he looked almost as shaken as she felt.

"Gross," Noelle muttered. "Why on earth did you two kidnap me from a perfectly decent vacation to make me watch this disgusting display of lewd middle-aged behavior?"

Del recovered quickly. "You're our chaperon, kiddo."

"Don't call me kiddo," Noelle said coldly, her eyes pinned on Del. "We're not going to bond or anything, so you might as well save your time and energy."

"No kiddo, huh?"

"No kiddo."

"How about I call you ladybug, instead?"

Noelle made a guttural noise that very clearly spoke of her distaste, before spinning around and heading for the kitchen.

Del smiled down at Vic. "I think she's beginning to like me."

Vic shook her head. "I'm sorry. She's really not always so…awful."

And no matter how much a kiss made her think otherwise, she knew Del would not be around long enough to get to see Noelle's better side.

Going to bed early was preferable to watching the two lovebirds. How incredibly *gross.*

Noelle kicked back on the bed, her eyes on the ceiling, her headphones and the music in her ears drowning out any sounds that might drift through her closed door.

This was bad. Really bad. Yeah, her mom did date now and then, but never guys like Wilder. She spent more time with her friends than with guys, especially Wanda Freeman. Wanda had even fixed her best friend

Vic up a few times, but that had always been a disaster. There were men from Grandpa's company, dweebs like that stiff James Moss, or that guy who smiled all the time, Ryan what's-his-name. She had never worried about those guys because they never kissed her mom like that, or went to a crappy shack in the woods on vacation or called her kiddo and Ladybug. She snorted. Wilder obviously thought if he played nice with the kid it would make a difference to the mother. Fat chance.

If only her Dad knew about Wilder, he'd do something. He'd come in and run that thug off and realize that the three of them belonged together again. It had been such a long time…she barely remembered what it was like to have a father *and* a mother. Her dad steered clear of her because her mother was always there, and that was obviously uncomfortable for him. It wasn't his fault that he rarely came around, or that when he did he didn't stay long. It wasn't his fault that he never smiled anymore, or that he was always so anxious to leave.

Yeah, if he knew, he'd do something. Noelle smiled. Something drastic. How cool would that be?

He wanted her. More than was right, much more than he should. Hell, he wasn't eighteen anymore. He didn't lose control of his emotions *or* his libido.

But he wanted Vic so much it hurt.

She stepped onto the porch to join him. The screen door squealed, the planks on the porch squeaked as she stepped across them. He felt each sharp sound as if it fluttered through his body. This was not good.

"She's asleep?" he asked.

Vic nodded as she sat in the rocking chair beside him. "Out like a light," she whispered, as if her voice might disturb the night. And what a night it was. The moon was full and the air had taken on a comfortable cool hint as it washed across the nearby lake and through the trees. The air smelled clean and fresh, the moonlight lit the rustic front porch and the woods before them. And it lit Vic in a way that made her look even more beautiful than she usually did. That in itself was a miracle.

He could not afford to get sloppy and sentimental over a woman. He tried to tell himself that what he felt was just a residual of what they'd had long ago, the faint echo of what an eighteen-year-old had thought was love.

And still, he wanted her.

"How long will you be here?" Vic asked, her voice soft and easy.

"As long as it takes."

"That's not—"

"Necessary?" Del interrupted. "No, I guess it's not. But what am I supposed to do, Vic?" Anger made his voice too caustic. "Leave you here?"

"I can take care of myself."

"Not this time."

Vic rocked, silent for a long moment. "Surely no one will find us out here. I'm sure Noelle and I will be fine on our own."

Was she so anxious to get rid of him? Apparently so. "Let's get one thing straight, Vic. I'm not leaving here until we have the Mayrons in custody. If I do have to leave, Shock will be here. No one else. I don't trust anyone but Shock." *With you.* He couldn't say that. He couldn't reveal that much of himself, to Vic or to anyone else.

Vic sighed, and he felt it. "If it was just me, I'd argue with you," she said. "But I won't take risks with Noelle. If there's even a remote chance those people will find us here…" She turned her head and looked at him, square on for the first time since he'd kissed her. "I'll do anything to keep Noelle safe," she said. "Anything."

He'd use that, if he had to. If she tried to kick him out again he'd appeal to her motherly devotion and protective instincts. "Good. Then we agree that I'm staying."

Again Vic sighed, and then she nodded her head.

That taken care of, his mind took a more personal bent. While he was making sure Vic was safe, he had to get her out of his head. He wasn't sure exactly how to do that. Concentrate on her faults and convince himself he was much better off without her? Remember the past and how much it had hurt?

Or sleep with her and get this obsession out of his system, once and for all?

More than once she'd tried to push him away, but she kissed as if she was interested. Very interested.

"Are you…seeing anybody?" he asked.

He felt her eyes on him but continued to stare out at the night. "No. Not at the moment."

Del nodded. Good.

"You?" she asked.

"Not at the moment."

He couldn't tell if her soft hum was one of approval or not. Maybe. Maybe.

"I always figured you'd be married by now. Have a few kids," she said.

So, she *did* think about him. "Nope. No time, I guess."

"You really should. Noelle is the best part of my life."

Del turned his head and looked at Vic, studied her moonlit profile. He wisely contained his first response—

You've got to be kidding. "I'll bet you're a great mother."

She smiled gently. "There was a time I thought maybe I was. The past couple of years I've had my doubts. I wonder if maybe Noelle wouldn't be happier if I'd done something different."

"We all rebel at that age, at least a little."

"I guess," she agreed in a low whisper. "Sometimes I wonder if I shouldn't have forgiven Preston, for Noelle's sake. Maybe I shouldn't have—"

"No," he interrupted, his voice sharp. "You deserve better than that, Vic. Much better."

She laid her eyes on him and smiled, gentle and confident and…every bit as stirred up as he was.

He didn't play games, not anymore. He didn't dance around delicate issues because he was shy or discreet. He'd never had either of those attributes.

"Vic, where am I sleeping tonight?"

Even in the moonlight, it seemed her face went pale. "You can have the bed," she said. "I'll take the couch."

Not exactly the response he'd been hoping for. There were two bedrooms. Noelle was sleeping in one. The other had a queen-size bed and its own personal bathroom. And then there was the sofa in the main room. "I'll take the couch," he said.

"It's too short for you," Vic protested.

"It folds out into a bed."

"Oh."

Yeah, he'd sleep on the couch tonight, and maybe even tomorrow night, but he had a feeling he wouldn't be there long.

Vic tossed in the bed, unable to get comfortable. Her nightgown twisted around her legs, frustrating her even

more. The mattress was too soft, then too hard. The air
in the confining room was too hot, then not hot at all.
But deep down she knew it wasn't the bed or the temperature that kept her awake. It was Del.

Where am I sleeping tonight? Why had he asked her
that question? It could have been taken more than one
way, but there had been nothing innocent about the tone
of his deep voice, nothing innocent about the look in his
eye as he'd asked that loaded question.

She'd been tempted, momentarily, to answer *With me.*
But she hadn't and she wouldn't.

For good reason. Del had lied to her, he'd almost gotten her killed, and he thought he could come riding in
here on his white horse and take over. She didn't need
him to protect her. She didn't need any man to protect
her.

More than all that, there was the issue of Noelle. If
Del knew she was his daughter he'd never be out of
their lives. He'd bring danger with him, the threat from
criminals like the ones who'd kidnapped and almost
killed her.

And then there was the danger to her heart, and
Noelle's. Preston's leaving had hurt Noelle and the poor
girl was still suffering. She didn't need another man
coming into her life, becoming a part of it and then
walking away. And that's what Del would do, in the end.
Walk away. Maybe she could survive the hurt to herself,
but to put Noelle through that again? She couldn't.

Del could never know Noelle was his daughter. And
Vic couldn't get involved with him and continue to lie.
It was too hard. So no matter what she wanted, no matter
how tempted she was…

Hot once again, she threw off her covers and sat up.

She hadn't been with or wanted a man in years. She was alone, and had been long before the divorce. Alone, but never lonely. She didn't mind that there was no man in her life. All she needed was her painting and her daughter. Life was simple that way. Simple was good. But Del made her feel lonely, as if she was missing something important. Something beautiful.

On bare feet, Vic slipped out of her room and down the hallway. Passing Noelle's door, she heard her daughter's deep, even breathing. As she neared the main room, she heard Del's deeper, decidedly masculine breaths.

Just a peek, that's all she wanted.

She stopped at the entrance to the main room and leaned against the wall. Del was sprawled across the sofa bed, which was indeed too small for him. He filled it, his feet hanging off the end, his out-flung arms and legs taking up the length and breadth of the mattress.

And that hair… She had always loved his long hair. It was beautiful and it suited him. Wild. Unconventional. He was definitely not the kind of man her father had envisioned for her.

He was definitely not the kind of man she needed in her life now. If she let him get too close, he would only complicate matters. But, oh, as she watched him sleep she wished again that when he'd asked *Where am I sleeping tonight?* she'd answered *With me.*

With a shake of her head she turned and silently returned to her bed. *Stupid,* she chided silently as she walked away. If she knew one truth, it was that Del Wilder was not for her and never would be.

Chapter 4

Del heard the steps, too cautious in the hallway. Noelle, he saw as he cracked one eye and caught sight of a young girl's legs topped in yet another pair of black shorts. Her toenails, he noticed, were painted a dark red. At least she had a color scheme going for herself.

It wasn't even seven in the morning, yet, and here she was, creeping through the cabin as if she had all sorts of nefarious plans. He had no doubt that *nefarious* was Noelle's middle name.

The keys to Vic's van were close, there on the coffee table he'd moved to the wall so the couch could be opened into an uncomfortable bed. He wondered if Noelle would be so bold, and pretended to sleep.

She came close but didn't go for the keys. Instead she snagged his cell phone from an end table on the other side of a fat chair and headed stealthily for the kitchen.

When she was out of sight, Del left the sofa bed with just as much stealth and followed. He'd slept in a pair of flannel pajama bottoms, too warm for summer but all he had. He grabbed a T-shirt from the chair he'd tossed it over last night and pulled the garment on as he walked.

Who was Noelle calling? A boyfriend? Her friend Michelle? He wasn't worried about her giving anyone directions to the place, attempting what she was sure to see as rescue. She'd slept most of the way to the cabin, dozing through the many twists and turns he'd taken to get here.

He was just about ready to jump out and give the girl a scare—no more than she deserved—when Noelle's soft voice stopped him.

"Dad?"

Something in his heart clenched. This was no tough teenager with a bad attitude; it was just a little girl who sounded uncertain and a bit afraid. Del leaned against the wall, out of sight, and waited.

"I...I know you're getting ready to go to work," she said quickly. "But—"

Preston must've interrupted, because Noelle went breathlessly silent once again.

"Mom has a boyfriend," she said, her voice too fast. Was she afraid her father would interrupt again? "A real loser."

Del relaxed against the wall. Loser?

"I can't stay here. They practically kidnapped me and forced me to go on vacation." She sighed. "Don't laugh! It's not funny. We're, like, in the woods, and I think they expect me to go fishing or something." She was silent for a short minute or two. "It's just gross."

Finally, she got to the point of her call. "Can't I come live with you?"

The tone of her voice was so tender, so fragile, Del

had the feeling—no, he knew—that Noelle had asked this question before.

"Just for the rest of summer vacation, maybe," she said in a lower voice. "Or…a couple of weeks."

She was definitely breathing now, too hard, as if struggling to stop the tears of rejection.

"Okay," she finally said. "Maybe I'll see you then. 'Bye."

At the moment, Del really wanted to get his hands on Preston Lowell. What a jerk. What a complete and total jackass.

He pushed away from the wall and stepped into the kitchen, stretching his arms over his head, closing his eyes as he yawned to give Noelle a chance to wipe away the tears on her face.

"'Morning, kiddo," he said as he dropped his arms.

She opened her mouth to argue.

"Noelle," he corrected himself quickly. "Good morning, Noelle. Did you get up to make me breakfast?"

To look at her, you wouldn't know she'd been crying just a few seconds ago. Tears were gone, eyes were dry and flinty. The cell phone had been quickly and expertly slipped up the long, baggy sleeve of her black shirt. "No."

"Then maybe I'll make you breakfast," he said, heading for the refrigerator.

"Don't bother." She looked angry, as if she wanted to take all her frustration out on him. But she didn't leave.

"You didn't eat much last night," he said. "You must be hungry."

Noelle's short cherry-red hair stood on end, and her face…she tried so hard to be tough as nails, unforgiving and obstinate. But there was still a touch of the child in her mouth and her eyes.

"What are you making?" she finally asked.

Shock had equipped the place well, and last night Del had searched all the cabinets, taking stock of their supplies. "Pancakes?"

"Okay." Noelle slipped out of the room for a moment, while Del took the pancake mix and a bowl from the cabinet. When she returned and took a seat at the round table on the opposite side of the room, he could see that she no longer hid the cell phone up her sleeve. If she hadn't already been jerked around once this morning, he'd let her know she'd been caught. Best to let her think she'd gotten away with swiping the phone, for now. He imagined conversation of any kind would be unwelcome at the moment, so he whipped up the batter without saying a word. As he dropped the first dollop of pancake batter onto the preheated griddle, Noelle shifted in her chair.

"You're wasting your time, you know," she said.

"Making pancakes?" he asked, glancing over his shoulder.

"Setting your sights on my mother," she clarified with a sharp glance.

"What makes you think I've set my sights on your mother?"

She rolled her eyes. "Please. I saw you kiss her. You kidnapped me and dragged me to the middle of nowhere for a *family* vacation. What is it, Grandpa's money? Hate to disappoint you, but he has it all. Mom pretty much told him to take a hike, years ago, so we don't exactly share the wealth. If you want to get your hands on the Archard fortune, you'll have to date Grandpa."

Del flipped pancakes. One kiss did not a sight-setting

make, but it was a simpler explanation than the truth. Still, it had been a great kiss, and if he had his way… "Maybe I like her," he said. "It doesn't have to be more complicated than that."

"She has lots of boyfriends," Noelle said sharply. "All of them better than you."

With his back to the girl, Del smiled widely. "Is that a fact? How could they possibly be better than me?"

"They have jobs, they wear suits. They cut their hair."

"I have a job, I own a suit and what's wrong with my hair?"

He headed to the table with a plate full of small pancakes. Without being asked, Noelle jumped up and went to the refrigerator for syrup and juice. "Nothing," she said as she returned to the table. "If you actually enjoy looking like a reject from the seventies."

Del gave her a big grin as he moved a stack of pancakes to his plate.

Annoyed that her plan wasn't working, Noelle lifted her chin and tried another tactic. "Besides, you don't want to get involved with my mother. She's psycho."

"Psycho?"

Noelle piled her own plate high. "Yep."

"Can you give me some examples?"

Noelle pursed her lips. "She freaks whenever I mention dating. I can only go out if it's a special occasion, a double date, and even then I have to go with someone she knows and approves of."

Del shook his head. "You're right. Psycho."

His sarcasm didn't get past her. "I was born on Christmas Eve and she named me Noelle Eve. Noelle Lowell, can you believe that? Everyone makes it rhyme. But I guess I should consider myself lucky. What if I'd been born on Easter, or Valentine's Day, or…Thanks-giving?''

"Little Turkey Lowell."

She stuck her tongue out at him.

"Noelle is a very pretty name," Del said. "Now, eat your pancakes."

She did, digging in and dismissing their conversation.

His breakfast finished, Del walked into the living room and collected his cigarettes from the end table. When he returned to the kitchen, Noelle had finished eating and sat there with her eyes on the window and the view beyond. She was, no doubt, thinking about her father and his refusal of her request. Poor kid.

When she saw the cigarettes in his hand, her eyes lit up. "Can I have one?" she asked.

"No."

Again, she stuck her tongue out at him. "Selfish."

"I just don't want your mother to, you know, kill me." He lit up, and Noelle rolled her eyes. "Besides," he added, "these things are not good for you."

"And they're good for you?"

"Think of me as a bad example."

Noelle pushed her chair back and gave him a glare that said she wished she could do murder, here and now. "Don't worry," she said. "I already do."

Vic dabbed at the canvas on the easel before her. The light here on the front porch was great, the scene before her was magnificent, but she couldn't make herself con-centrate on painting. Usually painting saved her, took her mind off of anything and everything. Not today. Del Wilder was stronger—pulled more effectively at her heart—than this vocation she'd lost herself in for most of the past fifteen years.

Even if the screen door hadn't squeaked, she would have known that Del was behind her. He charged the air with his very presence, he set every nerve in her body on alert.

"The kid's taking a nap," he said, his voice low. "She didn't like my suggestion that we take a hike this afternoon, and when I mentioned fishing instead, she told me to…" He took a deep breath. "Well, I think it's impossible, and even if it was possible it would definitely be unpleasant."

Vic set down her brush and turned to face Del. "I'm sorry. She knows better…."

"Don't sweat it." He flashed her a wide smile. "She's a good kid. Not at all like you were at that age, all sugar and very little spice, but still a good kid. Likes to stir up trouble, doesn't she?"

Vic found herself returning Del's smile. "Oh, yeah."

It would be so simple, right now, to say, "She's so much like you." But she didn't. Her mind was made up. Del was here, for a little while, but he wasn't staying. And he wouldn't have the opportunity to break Noelle's heart. Vic still wasn't sure about her own.

He walked closer, took her hand and stared down at the bandages on her fingers. "How are they?"

"Fine."

His head cocked up, his eyes met hers. "Really?"

Vic could only nod as Del lifted her hand and kissed the palm. Quickly. Sweetly. And that simple contact sent shivers through her body.

"I understand you're dating," he said as he dropped her hand.

The surprise must've shown on her face because Del's smile grew wider. "Lots of guys," he continued. "Who wear suits and cut their hair and have *jobs*."

"Noelle."

The twinkle in Del's eyes was the answer. "So, if I asked you to take a nice long walk in the woods, would I be stepping on some man's toes?"

"I'm not dating," Vic said, ignoring his offer of a walk in the woods. "I mean, I *have,* but…not lately."

"Why not?" She tried to return to her easel, but Del's hand on her shoulder stopped her. "Still in love with Presto?"

"No!" she said, too sharply. "God, no."

"You're a beautiful woman, smart, sexy. I can't imagine why there aren't guys crawling all over you."

Vic shuddered, just a little.

"Vic?" Del's voice was low, comforting.

She steeled herself and turned, tipping her face up to look him squarely in the eye. "Okay, you tell me why you never got married and I'll tell you why I don't date."

She meant to scare him away, but her ploy didn't work. His hand came up to touch her cheek, his eyes went dark. "Why didn't I get married? There are a few answers to that one." His fingers traced her jaw. "The job, for one. The job is consuming, at times, and it's never easy. Takes a special woman to handle what comes with it."

"Other law enforcement officers, even those who work undercover, they get married."

"Yeah, but it's hard to make it work."

"So that's why—"

"That's one reason," he interrupted.

Vic nodded. She should stop this, here and now. The last thing she needed was to be Del's confidante, to know and cherish his secrets. She said nothing to silence him.

"Kids," he said, smiling gently. "You get married, the next thing you know there are babies everywhere you look."

"You don't like them?"

"I like them fine, as long as they're someone else's," he teased. "I figure if I ever have kids they'll be just like me. Payback is hell."

It was the perfect time to tell him...maybe not.

"I suppose the truth is, the right woman just never came along." His smile faded. "I never met anybody who made me feel..."

She waited for him to finish. *The way you did. The way you do. Like this.*

But a moment later the lilt was back in his voice, and he finished. "Like shackling myself."

"Not looking for an old ball and chain," she teased, grateful he hadn't gotten more personal. This was tough enough.

Del shook his head. "No, thank you, ma'am. Your turn."

Vic took a deep breath. "I did date a few times, after the divorce. *Years* after the divorce, to be honest. Marriage to Preston was less than wonderful. Why would I ever want another man in my life?"

Del's blue eyes darkened. "Did he hurt you? I swear, if he did I'll take him apart."

"He never hurt me, physically. He just...broke promises. Lied. Made me feel like I was always, always wrong, no matter what I did."

One of Del's fingers brushed through her hair, a small gesture of comfort. She liked it. "He's just one man, Vic. We're not all like that."

She shook her head, not looking to argue, just wanting to get this over with. "I know that, but still... When I did date, I was always looking for the lie. What does this man really want? Why is he really here? I never dated any one guy more than three times.''

"You drove them away before they could hurt you."

She ignored that dead-on conclusion. "My father still tries to play matchmaker now and then. That's the worst, I think. It makes me feel like a little girl trying to live up to Daddy's expectations. The other attempts at dating weren't much better. Some of the men I never saw again, a couple actually became friends. But..." She stumbled, and her voice wouldn't come out right. This was not a discussion she could have with Del, of all people. She didn't want to be hurt again, and he had hurt her more than anyone else ever had or could. And he didn't have a clue.

"Vic," Del whispered, his lips moving toward hers. "Do you want to know why I'm here?"

She swallowed hard. "Because those kidnappers..."

He shook his head. "I could put an army of men on you and Noelle to keep you safe. I could hire a dozen bodyguards while I go out there and find Tripp and Holly myself. It's what I do," he added gently. "I like action, not baby-sitting."

"You can go..."

"I *can't*," he interrupted. "I can't go. Do you want to know why?"

Yes. More than anything. Tell me. "No." After all, it was safer that way, and Vic Lowell was nothing if not safe.

Her response did not deter him. He kissed her. He stirred her up, with a gentle kiss and a tender hand at her back and a silent invitation she ignored.

Somehow she ended up with her back against the wall

of the rough cabin, her legs slightly spread, Del resting between them as he kissed her. And she kissed him back.

It wasn't supposed to be like this. They weren't kids anymore. Hormones could be controlled. Desire could be tamed. Squashed down. Dismissed as what it really was—physical attraction.

So why couldn't she dismiss this?

Del backed away. A trickle of sweat ran down his face, down his neck. She felt a drop of perspiration tickle her spine.

"You always did drive me crazy," he said, giving her a crooked smile before turning his back on her and walking away.

Del lay on the torturous sofa bed, wide-awake even though it was almost two in the morning. He had to get out of here, the sooner the better. Like he'd told Vic this afternoon, anyone could keep an eye on her and Noelle until Tripp and Holly were caught. Anybody. Well, he wouldn't trust them to just anyone, but there were a large number of qualified bodyguards out there, available at a snap of the fingers.

So why was he still here?

After the kiss, things had turned awkward. Even after all this time, he knew Vic too well. She wanted him, but she didn't like the fact, and she was doing her best to deny it. In a way he knew how she felt. He hadn't been this confused in sixteen years, since Vic had stood there on the front porch of her big house and told him it was over. He hadn't seen it coming, and the blow had blindsided him. Nothing blindsided him anymore. His life was black and white, good guys and bad guys, right and wrong.

Physically, he wanted Vic. Emotionally, he was still

drawn to her in a way he could not explain. Nothing good could come of a relationship that went beyond bodyguard and woman in trouble. If they slept together, this was bound to end ugly.

And still he wanted her.

The reason for his confusion walked into the room, dressed in blue and moving without making a sound, like a tantalizing vision out of a dream.

"You can't sleep, either?" Vic asked as she came near the bed.

Didn't she know better? She knew he wanted her. Needed her. She had to know that the reason he was here when he could be hunting Tripp and Holly...was because he didn't trust anyone else in the world to watch over her.

"No," he said simply. "Can't sleep."

She started to sit down in the chair at the opposite wall, but with the crook of a single finger, Del invited her to sit on the side of his bed. After a moment's hesitation, she headed over his way, blue robe dancing as she walked, curling hair wild and inviting. He wanted to bury his hands in her hair, and that would just be the beginning.

Vic hesitated a moment, standing beside him, and then she sat. The thin, crooked mattress gave under her weight, and Del let himself roll toward her.

"What you said about getting someone else to watch us," she whispered, her eyes on a moonlit window and the darkness beyond. "I think maybe that would be a good idea."

"Why?"

"You don't want to be here, Del," she argued. "You'd rather be..."

"Here," he said, dismissing the confusion that had

kept him awake so late and focusing only on the present situation. "I'd rather be right here."

She looked down at him and her hand reached out to brush a strand of hair away from his cheek. "I don't understand this."

"Sure you do," he said, trying to make light of *this*. "I want you. In spite of yourself, you want me. We're not kids anymore, Vic. We understand that attraction and love are not the same thing. They're both nice, but they're not the same."

He leaned into Vic and kissed her lightly, then again not so lightly. She didn't hold back, or turn away, and eventually the tension in her body lessened. He felt the yielding first in her lips, then in her body. She drew her lips away, swollen and well kissed.

"I thought you were a memory," she said. "Nothing else, and now you're here and everything is…different."

"You've been fighting it."

She nodded.

"Tired of waging a losing battle?"

There was a hesitation, but again she nodded.

"Good."

He drew Vic down beside him and she didn't resist. The length of her body lay close to his, her head rested on his shoulder. When he felt her soft lips on his neck, he closed his eyes and savored the sensations that shot through him.

Since the moment Tripp had bound Vic to him, he'd wanted her just like this. Her body next to his, her mouth tasting, her hands touching. And reality was so much better than his daydreams. Warmer. Unexpectedly tender. He shouldn't want her so much, not after all this time, not after the way she'd sent him packing years ago.

But he did. Maybe if they got this *thing* out of their

systems, he'd be able to hand Vic over to someone else for safekeeping. She was like an itch he couldn't reach, a craving he didn't completely understand.

This was simple. He didn't need to understand much at all.

"Noelle," he said.

Vic sighed. "I looked in on her. She's sound asleep. Once she's out for the night, it takes a bomb to…" She stopped suddenly, then gave in to a small smile. "Poor choice of words, given the circumstances."

Had Vic made sure her daughter was asleep because she'd known she'd end up here in his bed?

With one hand, he untied her robe and parted the folds. The gown beneath that robe was modest, but the fabric was thin. Running his hands over her breasts he felt her body heat, the inviting softness, the pebbling of her nipples when he touched her.

She shook. With desire? Or because she was still a little bit afraid of *this?* He wanted to make sure there was no fear in Vic when he finally made love to her. He didn't want her to be thinking about anything but the way they came together, the need and the pleasure. Nothing else.

His own need was close to spiraling out of control. Every touch, no matter how delicate, made his blood pump harder and faster.

"Do you have a…a condom?"

"Yes," he said, laying his mouth on her throat, sucking gently.

"Where?" She shuddered, long and deep.

"In my suitcase."

"Maybe you should get it now."

He grinned as he rolled Vic over and towered above her. "Not yet."

His lips trailed down her throat to the valley between her breasts, where he lingered. Vic's hands threaded through the long strands of his hair, holding him to her, holding him tight. Her thighs parted. One leg hiked up, just a little.

He moved his mouth to a breast, brushing the fabric of her gown aside just enough to free the nipple he tasted, and sucked deep into his mouth. Vic moaned deep in her throat, the sound low and enticing.

"Maybe we should move to my bed," Vic whispered. "There's a door and…" She moaned softly. "It doesn't squeak."

"Maybe," he agreed. "But not right now. I'm not ready to let you go."

He touched her, arousing with fingers and the rough brush of his palm, relearning the curves and soft flesh he had once known so well. Vic did the same, running her hands over him, trailing her gentle fingers over his body. When her hand rested on his chest, above his heart, he was glad of the dark.

He wanted her now, hard and fast, but he took his time. Everything slowed. He tasted her, touched her, pressed his body to hers. He kissed her, again and again, and she kissed him back. Tentative at first, and then with abandon, as if she couldn't kiss hard or deep enough.

Her other thigh hiked up until she cradled him between her legs. Clothes still separated them, her panties and his flannel pajama bottoms, and still he could feel her. Hot. Ready. All he had to do was move a few inches of annoying clothing aside and he'd be inside her.

"Maybe you should get it *now*," she said again, more breathlessly this time.

"Maybe you're right."

Before he could move to collect the protection they

needed, he heard something that ruined the moment. A stealthily closed car door, outside the cabin. It was far enough away that he might think it was someone headed elsewhere—if it wasn't two in the morning and if he didn't know for a fact that there wasn't another cabin anywhere near this one.

Vic didn't hear it. Her arms and legs loosened, releasing him from their gentle grasp, and he rolled from the bed and headed for his suitcase. He came up not with a condom, dammit, but with Shock's Colt.

"Vic, baby," he whispered as he headed to the window and peeked through the curtains. He didn't see anything. Yet. "I want you to go to Noelle's room and lock the door, then I want both of you to get on the floor. Stay low, and don't leave that room or get off the floor until I come to get you."

She didn't waste any time doing as he asked, making her way silently out of the main room and into the hallway.

Chapter 5

Vic ran on bare feet to the end of the hallway. She didn't know what Del had heard to tip him off, but he'd heard something. Someone was out there. In the woods. In the dark. How had they been found?

"On the floor," Vic said breathlessly as she burst into her daughter's bedroom and closed the door behind her. She noticed with a sinking heart that there was no lock on Noelle's door.

"What?" A sleepy Noelle barely lifted her head from the pillow.

Vic grabbed her daughter's arm and pulled her off the bed. Noelle squealed as she slid across the sheets and off the mattress to tumble to the floor. With an accusing look in her eye, she nimbly worked herself into a twisted sitting position.

Sitting on the floor beside the mattress, knees up and spine resting on the side of the bed, Vic placed an arm around her daughter. Even in this dim light, with nothing but moonlight through the window, she could tell that Noelle's hair was an unnatural shade. Vic sighed and lightly touched one sleep-tousled strand.

"Mother," Noelle said, that indignant voice too loud in the dark.

"Quiet," Vic whispered, and Noelle complied.

Vic's heart beat too hard. She couldn't breathe deeply enough and her knees shook. Were her physical symptoms of stress caused by her fear, or by what she and Del had been doing before they'd been interrupted?

Her heart had started pounding, her knees had felt weak and her breath had been stolen away long before Del had heard the noise that alarmed him.

Her eyes remained focused on the doorknob. What difference did it make why she shuddered? All that mattered was keeping Noelle safe.

Vic strained to hear something. Anything. All was silent. Much too quiet. She scanned the room for something that might be used as a weapon in case someone other than Del came to the door. Nothing. Absolutely nothing. All they had was a window that opened onto the night and unknown, unseen dangers. And it might be their only choice.

"What's wrong?" Noelle whispered.

After this was over, she'd have to tell Noelle what had happened at the warehouse. Part of the truth, anyway. But for now, a simpler explanation would have to do.

"Del thought he heard someone prowling around the house."

Noelle sighed and relaxed, visibly relieved. "It's probably just a possum or something," she said, keeping her voice low. "Jeez, Mother, that guy is such a geek. Hasn't he ever been out of the big city?" Her jaw dropped as a new thought struck her. "Mother!" she whispered indignantly. "He's sleeping on the couch, right? So how did you know he heard something?" She took in the nightgown, the mussed hair. "Oh, Mother… this is so completely and totally disgusting."

"Noelle," Vic said in a low voice. "Can we have this discussion later?" Much later. Sometime like never. Again she searched the darkened room for a weapon of some kind.

What sounded like an explosion made Vic flinch and pull her daughter closer.

With a splintering *crack,* the wooden door flew back and crashed into the wall. Moonlight filled the cabin as Tripp quickly stepped inside, weapon drawn as he searched the room. Del had seen him coming and was waiting.

"Drop it."

Tripp swung his raised pistol in Del's direction, but he was too late. Del fired first and his bullet caught the crook in the chest.

The man who'd burst into the cabin fell, and half a second later Del was there to take the weapon out of the invader's hand. Tripp had tried to shoot Del with the Glock, the weapon he and Holly had taken at the warehouse.

"Tried to shoot me with my own weapon," Del said, hefting the familiar pistol in his left hand. "Not very sporting of you."

Tripp wasn't dead, but he wouldn't live long without medical attention. Del didn't have time to linger over the man who had kidnapped Vic. Holly was out there, somewhere, and it didn't matter how blond and sweet-faced she was. The woman was just as mean as her husband. Meaner, maybe.

Tripp had kicked the door in, attacking without stealth, coming in with his gun raised and hoping for surprise. What about Holly? Would she come flying through the back door with a scream and a raised weapon? Or had she already slipped the lock and entered the cabin quietly?

Del listened. All was silent. Tripp breathed, unevenly and with effort. If Tripp had come in the front door, Holly had probably taken the back. Del headed toward the kitchen, his eyes peeled for shadows that shouldn't be there, his ears tuned for something, anything, that might be out of place. The creak of a floorboard, or the sound of breathing from a room where there should be total silence.

If Holly was already in the house, why hadn't she run to Tripp's rescue? Those two had always been close. They'd started out small-timers, dealing drugs together while they were still in their teens. Newlyweds, then. A devoted married couple now. They watched each other's backs, and one never did anything without the other. They were, in their own way, strangely devoted to each other. If Holly was here Del would soon know it, because she'd do her best to kill him.

Del heard a scuff, the soft scrape of a shoe, on the back porch. Holly wasn't inside yet, but she had to know that Tripp was down. Two shots had been fired, and if Tripp had been the one to come out of it standing, he would've shouted for Holly to come on, or gone to the back door to let her in so they could finish the job—finish *Vic*—together.

With the Glock in one hand and the Colt in the other, Del took a lesson from Tripp and kicked the back door out, breaking the flimsy lock and surprising Holly, who stood just a few feet away. She lifted her head, and Del could see the brightness caused by the tears in her eyes. His weapons dropped, just slightly.

"Is he dead?" she asked softly.

"Not yet. Take it easy. Hand over the gun and let me call—"

She didn't allow him to go any further. Her gun hand snapped up and so did Del's. They both fired and jumped aside at the same time.

Del rolled off the porch and landed in the soft, damp grass. He heard Holly, just a few feet away, but he couldn't see her. Grass rustled, a bush shimmied. Nothing more. Here at the back of the cabin everything was lost in shadows, and the moonlight was little help. He held his breath and listened. Where was she?

His heart lurched. Vic.

Del jumped onto the porch and ran through the busted back door. He waited for the sound of gunfire, the impact of a bullet in his back, but nothing happened. Inside the house, all remained still and quiet.

"Vic," he called out softly as he sidled toward the hallway. "Stay where you are. Don't move. Have you heard anyone else in the house?"

A soft voice drifted to him. "No."

"Are y'all okay?"

"Yes."

He breathed a sigh of relief. "Okay. Stay put. I'll be right back."

Del went back out the kitchen door, searching for signs of Holly. If she got away, there was no telling when she'd be back, or who she'd bring with her. Now was the time to bring this to an end, once and for all.

His nerves on edge, he circled the house cautiously,

a weapon in each hand. Gradually his eyes adjusted to the dark, but Holly was nowhere in sight. Everything was quiet. Too damn quiet.

Something rustled to Del's left and he spun around to face the wooded area beyond the clearing where the cabin was situated. He trained his weapon there, scanning for a spot of color that didn't belong. Holly had been wearing a dark purple T-shirt. It was dark enough to blend in with the shadows, but it was also *purple*.

Whatever was out there moved again, and then took off running low and fast. It was some kind of critter, not too big. Just big enough to make a good, loud noise.

Moving cautiously, Del circled the cabin. The front door stood wide-open, but he could see nothing beyond. All was black. Portions of the porch were so dark he held his breath as he searched them. She could be anywhere. So why wasn't she coming after him? Holly wasn't known for her patience or her finesse.

He circled the cabin twice before entering the house, again through the kitchen door.

Del was about to creep into the hallway and make his way to Noelle's bedroom, wanting—*needing*—to check and make sure she and Vic were safe, when he heard another gunshot. This came from a decent distance and was followed by the slamming of a car door and a revving engine. He listened, to make sure Holly was escaping and not driving her car toward the cabin. Sure enough, the sound of the engine faded quickly.

He hated to let her get away, but he was damned glad he wouldn't have to be looking for her while he loaded Vic and Noelle into the van.

"Let's go," Del called briskly as he hurried down the hallway. "Get dressed and grab your purses, but don't take time to pack." He threw open the door and found

Vic standing before the tiny closet door, feet firmly planted, a curling iron grasped in one hand. When she saw him she opened the closet door and an agitated Noelle quickly exited. Vic put her arm around her daughter, while Noelle tried to look cool but couldn't quite pull it off. Something about the picture tugged at his heart. Or maybe the excitement of the moment was just getting to him.

Noelle's wide eyes dropped to his hands. "Mother, he has *guns*."

"I know." Vic laid the curling iron on the dresser, moving none too steadily. "Do as he says and get dressed."

"But—" Noelle protested.

"No buts," Vic interrupted. "I'll explain later."

"You'd better," Noelle said as she reached into a dresser drawer to withdraw a black outfit. "I'd say you have a lot of explaining to do, young lady." She actually smiled, enjoying her opportunity to turn the tables on her mother in spite of the tension in the air.

In the hallway, Noelle's door closed behind them, Vic looked up at Del. "Did you get them?"

"Shot Tripp. Holly got away. That's why we have to get out of here right now. She might come back, and if she does, she won't be alone."

Vic nodded gently.

"I'm going to call Shock," Del said, turning and heading for the main room. "Tripp needs a doctor, and we need another place to hide."

"It won't take me long to get dressed," she said, hurrying into her bedroom.

Del stepped into the main room and glanced toward

the open door. And froze. The door hung open, crooked and rustic, and moonlight spilled over bloodstained wood.

Tripp was gone.

"He's a *narc?*" Noelle leaned over the seat. Her horrified face was illuminated by the greenish light from the dashboard. "Oh, my God. A thug would be better. Mother, you can't date a *narc!*"

Del kept his eyes on the road. A good thing, since Vic was certain her van had never been pushed to this speed before. It flew along I-65, just her van and a lot of trucks in these early-morning hours.

But he did grin. "What's the matter, kid, afraid all your drug dealer friends will be scared off?"

"And we're not dating," Vic said, unable to help herself. Del spared a quick glance for her, and his smile died. "We're just friends," she finished.

Just friends didn't kiss the way they did, she knew. *Just friends* didn't come very, very close to making explosive, out-of-control love. It sounded nice, it made a great explanation for Noelle, but she knew for a fact Del Wilder was *not* her friend.

"You need new friends, Mother," Noelle said, dramatically throwing herself into the back seat. "We never had people shooting at us until *this* guy showed up." She sighed, deeply and with great emotion. "I could really use a cigarette."

"No," Vic said sharply, surprised to find her refusal echoed by Del's deeper voice.

Noelle grumbled. Vic made out a few words, *kidnapped, narc* and *psycho* among them. Eventually, sooner than Vic had thought possible, Noelle fell asleep.

"Where are we going?" she asked, staring at Del's stark, sharp profile.

"You might not like it," he said softly.

"I don't like a lot of things these days. Why don't you tell me, anyway."

He smiled crookedly but didn't take his eyes from the road. The grin didn't last. "The Mayrons are after us. Both of us. We can't be sure about Tripp, but we know Holly survived. That last shot she fired before she took off was probably a warning of some kind. Her way of saying *I'll be back.* Tripp could be dead or he might just be wounded. It doesn't matter. If he survived, he'll be spending some time laid up and Holly will continue without him. If he died, she's only going to come after us harder." He took a long, slow breath. "She won't come alone, Vic."

He wasn't telling her anything she hadn't already figured out for herself. "What does that have to do with where we're going next?"

"Noelle is not a part of this," he said, his voice lower than before. "I know you want to keep her close. I understand that. But by keeping her with us, we put her in danger."

Vic felt the blood drain from her face. She knew he was right, and still... "Who can I trust with her? Not Preston, not my father, certainly not a stranger." *Wanda.* "I have a friend—"

"No. I'll feel better if Noelle is somewhere no one will ever think to look for her. They grabbed you to get to me. We can't assume they won't grab Noelle, if they get the chance."

Vic shivered. She was damn tired of Del Wilder always being right! "I can't just leave her anywhere," she whispered.

"Trust me," Del said.

She shouldn't. She didn't depend upon anyone these

days, especially not any man. But deep in her heart she did depend on Del. She trusted him with her life and—most important—with Noelle's.

But with her heart? No.

"I want a gun," she said.

"What?"

"A gun." She stared at Del's profile. "When Tripp and Holly attacked the cabin I was sitting on the floor by the bed in my nightgown with no way to protect myself or Noelle. It was the most helpless feeling of my life."

"I can protect you—"

"You won't always be there," Vic interrupted. "I want a gun."

He sighed, obviously not liking the idea. "Fine. I'll teach you to shoot when we get the chance, and then maybe we'll get you a little pistol."

She remembered too well what it had felt like to stand before that closet where Noelle hid, with nothing to defend herself or her daughter except a cold curling iron.

"I want a big one," she mumbled as she turned her gaze to the window and the darkness beyond.

Del pulled into the rest stop and immediately spotted the car he'd been told to look for. He pulled the van in alongside the gray midsize sedan and glanced through the window to the driver. Shock.

Shock exited the sedan and circled around, his eyes searching the parking lot and the rest-stop entrance behind Del.

"How'd they find you?" Shock asked as Del stepped from the driver's seat.

"I don't know, but I want you to go over this van

with a fine-tooth comb. They tracked us somehow, and I don't like it.''

Shock glanced at Vic, who waited silently in the passenger seat, and then into the back seat, to Noelle. "Everything's set. By sunup the lab guys will be tearing that cabin apart."

"I want to know everything," Del said.

"You got it."

Noelle did not want to be roused. She grumbled and waved her hands to shoo away whoever was trying to awaken her. Finally, angry eyes flew open and she exited the back of the van.

Shock smiled and offered his hand. "Hi," he said. "Nice haircut."

"Who are you?" Noelle asked less than cordially.

"Shock. I'm Del's partner."

Noelle's eyes went wide, and she stared at Del and cocked her head to one side. "You're *gay?*"

"Not that kind of partner," Shock amended. "Though we did have to go undercover in this bar one time, and—"

"Shock," Del interrupted.

"Don't make him stop! It was just getting interesting," Noelle complained as Del ushered her into the sedan. She plopped into the back seat and leaned back. Almost immediately her eyes closed and she smiled. It was a very devious smile.

Shock opened the door and sat beside her, invading her space so that she very quickly scooted across to the other side. "What's with your hair, anyway?" he asked, sounding more interested than insulting. "It's, like, the color of a cherry Tootsie Pop."

"It just happens to be very fashionable," Noelle answered, only slightly indignant. "Not that I'd expect someone like you to recognize the fact."

"Hey," Shock said. "I'm cool. I have a tattoo."

"Really?"

Shock rolled up his sleeve and displayed his tribal-art tattoo for a very interested Noelle.

Before Vic could step into the car, taking her place in the passenger seat, Del snagged her arm and pulled her aside. Leaning back on the fender, he pulled her into a loose embrace.

"Are you okay?" he whispered.

She nodded, but he didn't quite believe her. She was trembling, gently but unmistakably, and wouldn't look him in the eye. And she wanted a gun. It was a gut reaction to what had happened, he knew that. He'd been shot at. He'd had to use his weapon, more than once. It was part of his job.

He couldn't see Vic with a gun in her hand. She painted. She made beautiful things. She didn't shoot people.

"Sorry we got interrupted." He leaned down to kiss her forehead, worried about how the events of the night had affected her, concerned that—like the kidnapping— this was too much for her. *Concerned!* Hellfire, what was he getting himself into? "Next time, I'll make sure we're in a place where we won't be disturbed."

Vic lifted her head and looked him in the eye. Even by the light of the street lamp above their heads, he could tell she was much too pale. Her hair was going every whichway, curling around her face and down her back. "Maybe there shouldn't be a next time."

Del absently brushed away a curl that touched her cheek. She was right. He knew it, she knew it and still… "Baby, there will most definitely be a next time."

After a moment of silent resistance, Vic laid her head against his chest. She didn't bother to argue with him.

"Where are we going?" she whispered against his chest.

"You'll find out soon enough."

He expected an argument but didn't get one. Vic just remained very still for a moment, and then—as Shock left the back seat of the sedan and stepped into the driver's seat of the van—she pulled away.

Shock waited. He wasn't going to pull out of the rest stop until Del was well and safely on the road.

Vic stood back and stared at Del. Hard. "I'm trusting you with my little girl's life," she said, her voice stronger than it had been before.

"I know that."

"I don't know what's going to happen from here on out, but I want you to know one thing." She didn't look scared anymore. Not at all. "Noelle comes first. Her safety is more important than mine. Her life is more important than mine, and if there comes a time you have to make a choice about who needs protecting?" She shook her head. "There is no choice. My little girl comes first."

"I hear you."

"Promise me," she insisted softly.

"Vic…"

"I'm not getting in that car until you promise."

Del sighed. "Okay. Noelle comes first. I got it."

"Promise."

Knowing it was the only way he'd ever get her out of here, he did.

Chapter 6

She'd managed to doze in the passenger seat for a while, but Vic opened her eyes as Del turned the sedan onto a long driveway. Once again, they were in the middle of nowhere. There was not much to be seen through her window; no highway, no tall buildings, not a man-made thing in sight. There was just a gently winding driveway lined with overgrown flowering bushes.

They'd left Alabama over an hour ago, and were now in rural Mississippi. Del had been cautious, sometimes driving in circles to make sure they weren't being followed. He assured her no one was tailing them.

Del made one last turn and the house came into view. For a moment Vic forgot the terrible events that had brought them here and admired the view. Oh, how beautiful. More than beautiful, this cottage in the middle of nowhere was somehow stirring. It was a home, a warm place to land after a hard night.

The ranch-style house was white with blue shutters,

and the front porch sported not one but two old-fashioned rockers. The flowers growing at the base of the raised porch were more well tended than those along the driveway, adding color and a sense of warmth. There were even lace curtains in the windows, she saw, as an early-morning breeze made those curtains dance.

It was a serene, picturesque place, until the front door opened and a woman stepped onto the porch.

Vic knew immediately who the woman was, even though it had been years since she'd seen her. Louise Wilder. Del's mother.

Louise must have been very young when she'd had Del. She had to be in her early fifties, at least, but could easily pass for forty, in her snug jeans and T-shirt. She had a great figure, carried herself like a woman who got her share of exercise and had black hair and blue eyes, like Del. Like Noelle. These days, her hair was not as long as her son's, but fell well short of her shoulders and curled softly around her face.

"Del," Vic said as he pulled the car close to the porch. "Is this a good idea?"

"Shock knows where she lives, but that's it. Her old address is listed on my official paperwork, and she's been here for years. Her last name's Kelsey now, so no one can make a connection that way. She remarried ten years ago." He nodded, almost in approval. "Nice guy who passed away a little more than two years ago. It would be extremely difficult for anyone to link her to me, and even if they do…" He planted cold blue eyes on her face. "The house has a first-rate security system, including a panic button that connects directly to the sheriff's department." He smiled tiredly. "And we can trust her."

Louise Wilder—Louise Kelsey—had been a bartender

when Vic and Del had dated. She'd been wild even then, not at all like the other mothers. Vic had been a bit fascinated, but then growing up without her own mother around had left her curious about anything outside the norm. Word was, Del's mother had once been an exotic dancer. Vic had never been sure if that was true or not, but the woman certainly had the face and the figure for it.

Louise came off the porch and gave her son a big hug. "Shock said I should expect y'all early. Biscuits are in the oven. We can sit down to a big breakfast in about ten minutes."

"Sounds great," Del said, turning to Vic as she opened the passenger door. "You hungry?"

Vic nodded as Louise released her son and took a step back. The smile didn't fade, but the light in her eyes did. Of course that light dimmed. Vic knew without a doubt that she would rip out the heart of anyone who hurt her child. And she had hurt Del years ago. She hadn't wanted to, he didn't know why, and after all this time it shouldn't matter. But Louise seemed to be holding a grudge. Vic couldn't blame her.

Noelle climbed out of the car, all coltish legs and mussed red hair that stood on end. "Where *are* we? Dammit, Wilder..."

"Noelle!" Vic chastised. "Language."

"Sorry," she said, sounding anything but apologetic. "But I didn't expect to wake up and find myself back in the boonies again! If this thug is determined to stash us somewhere *supposedly* safe, why can't it be in a nice hotel somewhere, with a swimming pool and room service and pay channels?"

Noelle didn't know yet that she'd be staying here on her own. They'd have to tell her soon, and it wasn't a conversation Vic looked forward to. Del didn't plan for the two of them to stay here for more than a few hours, so she'd have to have that talk with Noelle soon. She wasn't going to be happy about the new plan, but if Del was right and this was the safest place for Noelle, it didn't matter if she was happy or not.

Vic glanced at Del and his mother again, and found Louise staring at Noelle. She wasn't smiling any longer, and she no longer displayed a quiet mother's outrage with the woman who had broken her son's heart so many years ago. Louise looked at Noelle, and she *knew*. Of course she saw the truth in Noelle's face. In an instant, Louise saw what Del didn't. She saw him in his daughter.

Louise recovered quickly, either dismissing her suspicions as fantasy or deciding to play dumb. For now. "No swimming pool," she said, "and no room service. Here in the boonies you wait on yourself or you go hungry."

"Great," Noelle muttered.

"But I do have cable TV, and if you'd like I'll let you help with the horses."

Noelle's expression changed completely, from sullen to excited. For a split second she looked like a wide-eyed child again. "Horses?"

"Four mares," Louise said, turning and heading for the house. "Do you ride?"

Noelle's face fell. "No."

"Well," Louise said as she entered the house, "we'll have to remedy that."

"Cool!" Noelle said, eagerly following Louise into the house.

On the porch, Vic laid a hand on Del's arm. "You're sure she'll be safe here."

"Positive."

"Then why can't we all stay, just for a while?" She knew Del was right about the Mayrons coming after the two of them, not Noelle, but the thought of being separated from her daughter at a time like this scared her.

Del reached down and touched her cheek. "They found us at the cabin. Too fast and too certain. Tripp and Holly want *you.* Leaving you here would increase the danger in this house tenfold. I won't take that risk, no matter how small, with my mother, any more than you'll take it with Noelle. We're the ones they want. We're getting out of here this afternoon."

Vic nodded. Trusting any man didn't come easy for her, and allowing one to make decisions for her…she'd put that behind her years ago. But in this instance she didn't have any choice. She had to trust Del to know what was best. "Okay. Where are we going?"

Del hesitated. "I don't know yet."

Strange as that answer sounded, Vic accepted it without question.

Noelle would be safe here, and that would ease his mind and Vic's. Then, maybe, they could set about finding Tripp and Holly. What he really needed to do was stash Vic somewhere, but he hadn't been able to come up with any hiding place he could be certain was safe enough for her. He couldn't leave her here. If she was found, her very presence would put Noelle and his own mother in danger. She was the one they wanted, the one who had seen Tripp and Holly. He couldn't leave her alone, either, and no one would protect her the way he would. This was getting sticky.

Maybe he didn't want to leave Vic with anyone else because he had such plans for the two of them. Personal plans that had nothing to do with the Mayrons. Tonight, tomorrow night, all the nights to come. Well, all the nights until Tripp and Holly were caught. After that…

He had it bad, if he was allowing his personal feelings for a woman to interfere with the job. If this had happened to anyone else…anyone…he'd be out there hunting Holly and Tripp while a team of bodyguards watched out for the woman involved. But with Vic, he couldn't let go. Because he wanted her so bad he could practically taste her?

No, it was more than wanting Vic that made him determined to stay close. Deep inside, he knew he could keep her safer than anyone else in the world, and like it or not she was his to protect.

Del stepped onto the back porch, lighting a cigarette as the kitchen door swung shut behind him. Vic and his mother had very little in common, but neither of them would allow him to smoke in the house.

"You could share," a petulant voice called from the other end of the porch.

Del dipped and cocked his head to look that way, and found a black-clad Noelle leaning against the house as she stared at him. She was excited about helping with the horses and learning to ride, but at the same time she was not pleased to be left behind. The word *abandoned* had come up often while Vic had tried to explain why it was best for Noelle to stay here.

"You're too young to smoke." Del walked down that way, his boots clipping against the weathered wood of the back porch. "And trust me, it's addictive."

Noelle smiled, somehow sweet and demonic at the same time. "I know. When you go for more than two hours without a smoke, you start to sweat."

"You don't want to get to the point where you have

to have these things.'' Del took the smoking cigarette from his mouth and wagged it at her. ''They're expensive and nasty and once you get hooked it's tough to go back.''

''Maybe I'm already hooked,'' she said, chin high and defiant.

''You're not sweating,'' Del teased.

In answer, she stuck out her tongue.

Del leaned against the wall beside her. ''You really smoke?''

''Yes.''

''Regularly?''

''Every day,'' she said. Chin up and eyes elsewhere, she was obviously lying. ''But lately I've been dragged from one isolated prison to another, and since either my mother or you have been on my back the entire time and there's absolutely no one else around, I haven't had the chance to bum a smoke. It's driving me crazy.''

Del took his cigarette between two fingers and offered it to her. ''Okay. Have a puff.''

Noelle curled her lip. ''Yew! You had that in your *mouth!*''

''If you were really addicted you wouldn't care whose mouth it had been in.''

Noelle screwed up her nose, crinkled her eyes and did something strange with her mouth, silently telling him otherwise. Well, she did have an expressive face.

Del took a nice, long drag and blew the smoke out slowly. ''How about a bet?'' he asked, flicking what was left of the cigarette to the porch and stepping on it with the toe of his boot.

''What kind of a bet?''

''We quit, both of us. Whoever caves and smokes first loses.''

"What if I don't want to quit?"

"You haven't even heard the terms yet."

Noelle shrugged, and Del continued. "If I win, we go out to dinner. Pizza and a movie, maybe."

"A date with you," she muttered. "That's brutal."

"And you wear something pretty," Del said with a grin. "Something *pink*."

"Yew."

"You wear that pretty pink ruffly dress I saw hanging in your closet."

She snapped her head around and glared, hard. "You were in my *closet?*"

"Very briefly."

"I can't believe you were in my closet! Isn't that, like, illegal or something? You snoop!"

"I wasn't snooping," he said. "I was…" Looking for bad guys wasn't a comforting answer. "Okay, I was snooping."

She forgave him, apparently, with a snort. "I hate that dress. Mother gave it to me for Christmas, and it's absolutely gruesome."

"I thought it was very nice." But he also knew it was not the kick-ass style Noelle had adopted for herself these days.

"What if *I* win."

"I have this great leather jacket at home. The weather's too hot for it now, but come winter…" He smiled and nodded. "You'd love it. It's black, and perfectly broken in. Soft as butter. I love that jacket."

Noelle grinned. "You do?"

"Yep." He could see the wheels turning behind Noelle's pretty face.

"Since you've been addicted much longer than I have, this is going to be way too easy."

Del offered his hand. "Deal?"

Noelle laid her hand in his. "Deal."

Del shook his head as their hands fell apart. "Even I wasn't smoking at fourteen. Does Vic know?"

Noelle's jaw dropped. "Fourteen? *Fourteen?* Do I look fourteen, you moron? I'm *fifteen.*"

"You'll be fifteen," Del said. "Christmas Eve."

The girl's head shook vigorously. "No, I'll be sixteen on Christmas Eve. *Sixteen.* Did you really think I was only fourteen or are you just yanking my chain again? God, Wilder, you are such a geek."

Del didn't hear anymore, even though Noelle's mouth continued to move. He heard and felt his heart beating as Noelle's words fell into place, but everything else became a dull, deep roar.

When Vic had stood on the front porch of her big white house and told him to get lost, better than sixteen years ago, she'd been pregnant. He stared at Noelle and saw the things he should've seen before. She had his eyes, and beneath that atrocious red dye she had black hair; he'd seen the pictures, he just hadn't been paying close-enough attention to details.

Not paying attention to details could get him killed, he knew that.

Noelle, with her smart mouth and her attitude, was too much like he'd been at fifteen.

His eyes, his hair, his defiance.

His daughter.

"Okay, are you already having withdrawal pains?" Noelle waved a hand in front of his face. "Hello?"

"Sorry," he said, his voice too low. "I was thinking about something else."

"Get that jacket ready, Wilder. I figure it'll be mine before sundown." She smiled, wide and wicked.

Del turned his back on her and went inside through the kitchen door. He pushed down everything that welled up inside him—emotion, anger, wonder—and looked for his mother. He found her trimming the yellowing leaves from a plant in the den.

"We're going now," he said, his voice too gruff.

"All right," she said, serene and accepting.

There had been a time when his mother had been anything but serene. Her life had been hard for a while. Del's father had left before he was born and a young Louise Wilder was left to raise a child on her own. She hadn't always made the best decisions, but her heart had always been in the right place. She was strong, like him. Like Noelle. She had bounced back and made a good life for herself.

"Shock said you and Vic probably wouldn't stay long." She continued to look at the plant. "I knew you were bringing her with you, but I was still surprised to see her. She hasn't changed much."

"No." He could not stand here and talk about Vic, not now. "Take good care of the kid," he said. "And don't let her get to you. She'll try."

"I managed with you, didn't I?" His mother turned, smiling widely as she set her scissors aside. "Noelle might be tough, but I'm tougher."

He nodded, once.

"Del?" Her smile faded. "Is there something you'd like to tell me?"

The truth hit him. Not as hard as it had a few minutes ago, when he'd realized that Noelle was his child, but it was a blow that made his heart hitch all the same. His mother had looked at Noelle and seen the truth he'd been blind to. She'd looked at her grandchild and recognized all the signs he had missed.

There was no way he could have this discussion with her here and now. "Not yet."

"Okay." She headed for the kitchen, head high. "But you two are not leaving until you've had something to eat. Neither of you ate enough breakfast, and you're not getting on the road without some lunch."

He couldn't possibly eat. "I'm not—"

"I don't care if you're hungry or not," she said as she disappeared into the hallway. "Go wake Vic," she called. "She's sleeping in the guest bedroom."

Del walked into the hallway and looked at the closed door Vic slept behind. What now? Did he play it cool? Pretend he didn't know that Noelle was fifteen, not fourteen as Vic had told him? Or did he wake Vic from her nap and confront her with her lies?

There had been too many lies since she'd come back into his life. He hadn't told her about being with the DEA, until he'd had no choice. She hadn't told him about the divorce, until she had to. Small, awkward lies. Truths withheld, until the right moment. But this thing with Noelle—telling him she was fourteen, not telling him that he had a daughter—they were too big to brush aside, too important to forget.

He threw the door open, allowing it to bang against the wall. Vic, startled by the noise, shot up. Hair wild, borrowed T-shirt molded to her body, she looked too good, still.

"Time to go, baby."

Vic studied her fingernails and bit her bottom lip. Leaving Noelle had been difficult, even though she knew it was for the best. They weren't fifteen minutes down the road, and twice she'd had to push down the urge to order Del to go back.

Del was probably planning their next move. He'd been quiet. Hadn't said a word since they'd left his mother's house. His eyes remained intent on the road before the speeding sedan; his jaw was clenched. She wanted to ask him where they were going, what would happen next, but there was something about the unrelenting expression on his face that stopped her.

Having Noelle with them to this point had been like having a chaperon. And still they'd managed to kiss. Twice. And last night she'd been swept away by the way Del touched her, and if Tripp and Holly hadn't arrived, she and Del would have made love on that creaking, uncomfortable sofa bed. She knew nothing could come of this. Of *them*. And still she felt like she'd been robbed of one of life's special moments.

So what would happen tonight?

She was allowing her emotions—no, her passions—to color her judgment. Del wasn't going to stay. He couldn't. They had less in common now than they had sixteen years ago, and he brought danger with him. Danger for herself she could handle, but when it came to Noelle…no amount of happiness for herself was worth putting Noelle in even the tiniest amount of danger. She'd dedicated her life to her daughter, and Del wasn't going to change that.

And yet, she found herself looking forward to tonight. Wondering what would happen, now that their chaperon was gone.

Less than half an hour after they left his mother's house, Del pulled the car sharply off the road. The car jerked and bounced as he left the pavement. The shoulder of the road was wide, and they hadn't seen another car for miles. They were all alone.

With the car in Park and the motor still running, Del

turned to look at her. The muscles in his face and neck were strained, and so was the hand on the steering wheel. He laid cold eyes on her face, and she shivered.

"Were you going to tell me?" he asked.

Her heart climbed into her throat. "Tell you…what?"

"How many secrets are you keeping, Vic?"

"Del…"

"Just the one, I'm thinking." His voice was tight with anger. "The big one. Did you think I wouldn't find out? That somewhere down the line I wouldn't discover that Noelle is not fourteen, she's fifteen?" He cocked his head slightly. "Christmas Eve. She was a couple of weeks early, wasn't she?"

"Yes." The word was so soft, she wondered if he heard it.

"Did you know you were pregnant when…" He pulled his eyes from her face and looked out the window. "When you sent me packing, did you know?"

Vic shook her head and muttered, "No. I swear, Del, I had no idea."

"And when you did find out?"

"You were already gone," she said softly, remembering that day too well.

"Dammit, Vic." He shook his head and glanced toward her again. "Why didn't you tell me?"

"You were gone…."

"Now!" he exploded. "Not then, not sixteen years ago. At this particular moment I don't give a damn about anything that happened sixteen years ago! Why didn't you tell me *now?* You could have told me when we thought we were going to die, or on the way to Gulf Shores to pick Noelle up, or even after I'd met her." His lips thinned; a muscle in his jaw twitched. "You could have told me last night. It's not like you haven't had a chance to come clean.''

The words caught in her throat.

Del gave her a crooked, bitter grin. "Don't tell me. You were waiting for the right moment. You wanted to do something romantic and sentimental and sweet. I know," he said, his voice low and dark, "you were waiting for Father's Day.''

"No," she whispered.

"Then what the hell were you waiting for?"

She'd told enough lies, she imagined. Another one wouldn't help matters any. "I didn't plan to tell you at all."

For a moment, Del looked like she'd slapped him. Finally he shook off the surprise and the hurt and put the car into gear. Vic reached out to lay a comforting hand on his arm. If he'd just let her explain—

He didn't move or shrug off her hand, but he glared at her. "Don't touch me," he ordered.

Vic let her hand fall away as Del pulled the car, too fast, onto the road.

Chapter 7

His shock faded and turned into pure, white-hot anger. Why was he surprised? He had never been good enough for Vic, he was certainly not good enough to be her child's father. At least she'd been honest about one thing. She hadn't planned to tell him, ever. It was apparently better to let Noelle think that a man who dismissed her when she called begging to live with him, who made her cry by brushing her off, was her father.

For all intents and purposes, in every way that mattered, Preston *was* Noelle's father. He'd been there when she was born, watched her grow, played Tooth Fairy and Santa Claus. If he'd ever been a decent father to her, he'd dried her tears and helped her learn to read and helped her with her homework. Those were the important things about being a parent.

He'd missed it all, and dammit, it hurt. More than he'd expected it could, more than it should.

Two rooms in the seedy motel he'd chosen for the

night would be best. A little distance, a wall or two between them, was definitely called for. But he didn't want Vic out of his sight. Not yet. At least there were two beds in this motel room. He'd even let her have the one that didn't cant to one side on a busted leg.

It was getting late in the afternoon. They might have driven farther on down the road, gone in a direction where Holly and her wounded husband wouldn't ever think to look, but this is where he wanted to be. He was close enough to Birmingham to keep in touch with the investigators and close enough to Huntsville to get there in an hour or so if he needed to. He and Vic weren't going to hide indefinitely. They needed to get this over with so he could get her out of his life. For good, this time.

Vic was in the bathroom, and had been for almost twenty minutes. She wasn't sick, he knew, she was hiding. Smart girl.

When his cell phone rang he grabbed it from the bedside table. This is what he'd been waiting for.

"Wilder."

"Tripp's dead," Shock said with no further introduction.

Del nodded and sat on the side of the canted bed. "I knew I hit him hard."

"Sorry, man, it wasn't your bullet that killed him."

A tickle of warning crawled up Del's spine; he knew he wouldn't like what was coming.

"Tripp's body was found less than a from mile the cabin. In addition to the wound in the chest, he had a bullet put through the back of his head," Shock explained. He finished with a low sound effect that whistled through the phone. *Kapow.*

No, Del didn't like this at all. "Holly never would've

done that. I don't care how bad he was hurt, how dangerous it would have been to take him to a doctor.''

"I know."

"There's someone else involved."

"Yep. Lab guys place three bad guys at the scene last night. And two blood types. Tripp's inside the front doorway and across the porch, where he apparently crawled to the step and then managed to get on his feet, and a few drops of another type on the back porch. You didn't get hit, did you?''

"No. I must've winged Holly." Maybe that's why she'd taken off, instead of coming inside and finishing the job. "I really don't like this."

"I've just gotten started," Shock said, his voice low. "Man, none of this is good news." He paused. Took a deep breath that echoed through the phone lines. "We know how they found you. There was a very sophisticated tracking device on the back of the license plate on Vic's van.''

Tripp and Holly didn't use tracking devices. Their methods were crude. Simple. This thing stunk to high heaven. "Great," Del mumbled.

"I made a quick trip to Huntsville this afternoon and checked out Vic's garage. There's an identical device on your Jag, and Del..." Shock paused for effect. "It wasn't there when I checked out your car after the warehouse exploded. It must have been added that night.''

That night, while he and Vic slept, someone had crept into her garage and planted those tracking devices. After he'd assured Vic that her house was safe, after he'd promised her that the couple who had kidnapped her was well down the road, someone who knew they were still alive had been right under their noses, planning for the next step. Making sure they wouldn't go anywhere without being tracked.

He'd been so damned certain that Tripp and Holly were a long way down the road and blissfully unaware that their plan had failed, that night. He knew them, knew how they thought. How they worked.

In his gut he knew he hadn't been wrong. Someone besides Tripp and Holly had planted those tracking devices. Someone who apparently didn't want to get his or her hands dirty by breaking into the house and finishing the job then and there. If Tripp and Holly had been at Vic's house that night, that's exactly what they would have done.

"This complicates matters," he said, keeping his voice low. He didn't want to have to explain these complications to Vic, not now. In truth, he still didn't want to speak to her at all.

"Yeah, if there's one more bad guy there might be two. Or three. Or—"

"I know," Del interrupted.

"So now what? I mean, we figured if we got Tripp and Holly, this was done. But if they're just hired help, we have a much bigger problem."

"Yes, we do."

"Do you want me to call Sinclair? Maybe Malone?"

"Not yet."

His own personal *much bigger problem* walked out of the bathroom, laid her eyes on him for a fraction of a second and then dropped them and sat delicately in the single chair in the room.

"Do you have a report from the guys in Mississippi?"

Vic's head snapped up when he said *Mississippi,* and her eyes lit on him again. They stayed this time.

"Yeah. All's well. As of an hour ago, your mom was giving Noelle riding lessons. Everything's cool there."

"Good. Call me if anything else comes up."

They ended the call, and Vic took a deep breath he somehow felt, all the way over here on the other side of the room.

"You're having them watched," she said.

"Yeah. A patrol car drives by the house a couple times a day."

"You didn't tell me you had men checking on Noelle and your mother."

He shrugged. "I was afraid you'd worry, think I had a reason for putting them under surveillance."

"Do you?"

"It's just a precaution."

No one could find Noelle at the Mississippi house. The daily reports were for his own peace of mind.

"Del," Vic said softly.

His nerves were on end, the way they were toward the end of an assignment, when everything was about to come down. He couldn't take this. If Vic sat there with her hands in her lap, all placid and reasonable, and tried to explain away the lies, he would explode. Fortunately, she didn't try to reason with him. "I need to go shopping."

He shook his head in disbelief. "Shopping?"

"I need to pick up a few things."

"My mother loaned you a couple changes of clothes."

Anger made her eyes spark. "I'd like some deodorant, my own underwear, a scrunchy to pull my hair back and some aspirin."

"Headache?"

"Yes," she snapped. "We left that cabin with nothing

but the clothes on our backs, and I don't see that a quick trip to Wal-Mart is going to draw out those two.''

He didn't tell her that he now knew there were more than two bad guys looking for them, or that one of the criminals who had kidnapped her was dead...she had enough to worry about. The car Shock had provided last night was clean; no one had been tracking them today. A quick trip to the store probably wouldn't hurt.

And just about anything was better than being stuck in a motel room with Vic.

Vic tossed her plastic bags onto the bed as Del closed the door behind him. ''I can't believe you wouldn't let me use my credit card,'' she said, still angry. ''It took almost all the cash I had in my purse to pay for this.''

''Using your credit card at this point would have been a little foolish.''

She spun on him. ''Foolish?''

He stared her down. ''Yeah. More than a little, to be completely honest.''

She couldn't win an argument with him, so she took her purchases out of the plastic bags and began to put them away. ''Sorry if I don't know all the rules about hiding from the world, like you do,'' she said beneath her breath. ''Can criminals even get my credit card information? And if they could, wouldn't it take some time?''

''Better safe than sorry.''

''My lifelong motto,'' she mumbled.

''What?''

''Nothing.'' It was true, though, and hearing the words made it all too clear. She'd lived her entire life *safe*. She'd sent Del away, married Preston, spent too many years trapped in a bad marriage...and all because it was the easiest way out. Suddenly she felt ashamed for always being so damned compliant. For letting other people guide her, as if she couldn't make up her own mind. It had cost her Del, it had robbed her of too many years of her life…and now it was going to cost her Del all over again.

She put away her purchases, taking the top drawer of the single chest in the room while Del dropped his own bag on his bed and made a quick phone call. He checked on his mother and Noelle again and apparently got a satisfactory report.

When everything was put away, Vic sat on the end of the bed and pulled her hair back and up, into a ponytail high on her head. It felt good to have the hair off her neck. Cool air washed over the too-warm skin there. It was soothing, in a way she had not expected. A small pleasure when everything else was falling apart.

"Are we going to talk about it at all?" she asked softly, without looking directly at Del.

"Talk about what?" He remained angry, coiled tight and untrusting, and she couldn't blame him.

"Noelle." She tilted her head and looked at Del, who took out a cigarette, played with it a moment, and then returned it to the pack and his pocket.

"What's to talk about?" he asked gruffly.

"Don't you want to know…anything?" she asked. "Don't you want to know how she's like you, and what her first word was, and what her favorite food is, and—"

"Why?" he interrupted sharply. "According to you I don't even deserve to know she's mine."

"I never said you don't deserve to know," she whispered.

He looked at her then, hard and unflinching. "You

admitted it yourself, you weren't going to tell me. Not now, not ever.''

"Of course I wasn't going to tell you," she said, her voice rising slightly. "If there are criminals out there who would go to the trouble to track me down, what would they do if they knew you had a daughter? For God's sake, Del, I've spent the past fifteen years doing everything possible to protect Noelle. I've dedicated my life to raising and protecting *your* child. She always comes first.'' She felt her temperature rise, her heart thud. No, she had not planned to tell him anything, but now that he knew... "There were too many mornings that Noelle was my only reason for getting out of bed. Some days I put one foot in front of the other only because she was there. Would I lie to you and everyone else to keep her safe? You bet your ass I would.''

He raised his eyebrows slightly, in obvious surprise, but then he hadn't ever seen her angry. Not like this. She had always been ice, not fire. Reason, not emotion. The Archards didn't raise their voices. That's what her father always told her.

"That's what this is all about?" he asked softly. "Keeping Noelle safe?"

"Yes."

He wasn't buying it, not entirely. "You don't think I'm capable of protecting my own child. You don't think I should even know she's mine.''

"Because I love her more than anything on this earth. Because I love her so much I would give my life to protect her.'' She wondered if Del wanted or needed to know that part of the reason she loved Noelle so deeply was because she was his. It only took her a moment to make the decision to keep that information to herself.

Del shook his head. "You should have known I'd

eventually find out Noelle was a year older than you told me she was." He seemed calmer, but not by much. At least he no longer looked like he was wound so tight something was about to pop.

"I didn't think you'd be around long enough to find out." It was true—she'd expected Del to waltz in and out of her life without ever knowing that Noelle was his child. Without ever having the chance to break his daughter's heart.

"Are you going to tell her? Ever?"

Vic's heart climbed into her throat. She almost answered *no,* quickly and decisively, but something stopped her. "I'm not sure." She shook her head gently. "A few days ago I knew the answer to that question, and I had no qualms about it. As far as Noelle is concerned, Preston is her father."

"And yet when you were trying to think of a safe place for her to hide, Presto wasn't even an option. You don't trust him, do you?"

Vic shook her head. She didn't trust Preston. Had she ever?

Del gave her a smile that held no warmth, no hint of humor, as he reached out and snagged his own bag of purchases. "Can I trust *you?*"

"Yes," she whispered, wanting more than anything for Del to trust her again.

He reached into the bag and came up with a pair of scissors. "With these?"

Del sat perfectly still as Vic cut away the long strands of hair. She'd been hesitant at first, snipping cautiously. She'd even held her breath on occasion. He'd known because he'd heard her. A soft intake, a long pause, a snip of the scissors and then she'd exhaled slowly.

But once she got under way, she put aside her caution and got into her role as beautician. She ran her fingers through his hair, cut quickly and mercilessly, and tossed what she could into the small trash can at her side. Even so, she missed some strands that drifted to the floor. Every now and then Del glanced into the garbage can. That was a *lot* of hair.

"Why are you doing this?" Vic asked as her cutting slowed. She took her time, once again, searching for imperfect and uneven places, brushing her tender hands through what was left of his hair.

"When you're on the run, changing your appearance now and then is always a good idea."

"So you've done this before? Cut your hair short?"

"No," he admitted.

"Seems a shame," she said softly. "You have such beautiful hair."

He was tired of the lies, large and small. When he worked undercover, his entire life was a lie. In his personal life, he couldn't abide them. "Noelle said I looked like a reject from the seventies," he said.

"That's why you're cutting your hair?" Vic sounded surprised.

"Not entirely, but it did cross my mind when I decided that I'm not going to sit around and wait for Holly to come after us. Come tomorrow, I'm heading into her territory." Sitting around and waiting, with Vic underfoot, was no longer an option. "With short hair and the geeky clothes I picked up, it's less likely that I'll be recognized."

Vic ruffled her fingers over his head. "I didn't think I would like your hair short, but I do," she said softly. Her fingers brushed against his neck, which was exposed for the first time in years. He couldn't remember when he'd last felt cool air there, the way he did now.

He hadn't looked in the mirror yet, didn't really want to until the chore was finished. He could only hope Vic was a better barber than Noelle's friend.

Just a few hours ago, he'd told Vic not to touch him. And with good reason. He'd never been so angry, and he wasn't going to stand for Vic trying to charm and cajole her way out of this one. She wouldn't soothe him with a hand on his arm, a caress to his cheek, those calm eyes of hers. He didn't want to be soothed.

But she had her hands on him now, her fingers on his neck and in his hair, a soft palm occasionally resting on one shoulder. She had such great hands; talented, gentle, easy hands that said with a touch what was in her heart. Well, if she'd *had* a heart…

"There," she said. "Finished."

Del stood and turned and looked at his new haircut for the first time. Unlike Noelle's new cut his was symmetrical, which was good, and while it was short, it wasn't *too* short. Vic hadn't given him a flattop, anyway.

"Well?" she prompted.

"It'll do."

"You're welcome," she said, just a little testy. And then she sighed, long and soft. "So when you're out there tomorrow looking for Holly, where will I be?"

"Here," he said without looking at her.

"Oh, no." She shook her head. "I'm not staying here by myself. I'm not…" She wrinkled her nose in distaste. "I'm not going to sit around and hide under the bed and wait for someone with a gun to knock on my door again. I did that once and I didn't like it. Speaking of guns, where's mine? You said you'd get me a gun."

"Haven't you given that up yet?"

"No, and I'm not going to give it up. I want a weapon I can protect myself and Noelle with."

"Noelle's not here."

"But you can't promise me that one day when she is with me I won't need to protect her."

"You haven't had need of a gun before."

"You weren't around before," she countered.

He wanted to argue with her...but he didn't have the patience. "We're getting off the subject. Can't we just have one argument at a time?"

"Fine. If you're going out looking for the criminals who kidnapped me, why can't you take me with you?"

Del laughed. "Yeah, right."

"Well, why not? I'm just as much a part of this as you are, and I don't see why I can't—"

"No," he said, his refusal more forceful than before. "You're staying here."

Vic smiled. "No, I'm not. You can leave me here, I suppose, but you can't make me *stay* here."

He leaned down and placed his nose close to hers. "What are you saying?"

"I'm just saying that I'm not staying here in this room or anywhere else all alone."

He opened his mouth but didn't get far.

"And I don't want some agent or cop or hired bodyguard I've never met, someone I don't know, to babysit while you go out and play the hero."

Again he tried to respond, but she cut him off. "I don't want Shock playing bodyguard, either. He gives me the willies."

Del raised his eyebrows. "Shock gives you the willies? Why?"

"The way he looks at me sometimes." Vic wrinkled

her nose. "Like he knows something about me that I don't. It's creepy."

She had no idea.

"Shock is—"

"No."

He'd had just about enough of her arguing. Time to pull out the trump card. "Fine. If you tag along with me, play cops and robbers and end up getting yourself killed, who's going to take care of Noelle?" He knew this was her weak spot. She'd already said she didn't trust her father or Preston Lowell with the kid. She'd safeguard herself for her daughter, she'd do anything...

"Your mother," she answered softly, taking him completely by surprise.

Chapter 8

Vic stared at the ceiling, mentally tracing the sharp line that marked the shadow cast by the more-than-halfway closed bathroom door. She needed to sleep, her body was exhausted. But no matter how she tried, she couldn't relax enough to even drift toward sleep.

She didn't think Del slept, either. His breathing wasn't deep and even enough, and there wasn't so much as a hint of snoring. Just…silence.

She should tell him, right now, that she'd changed her mind. When morning rolled around she'd stay here, thank you very much, with the doors locked and her ears opened for any sound that shouldn't be there. She'd sit here and wait for his return, and maybe if she was lucky he'd leave her armed, even though in truth she had no idea how to fire a gun. Yes, she could sit here, some well-armed cop in a car out front, maybe her own gun in her hand just in case, while Del did his job and went after the bad guys.

There were a couple of problems with that plan. She was tired of sitting around waiting for life to happen, and she was terrified that if Del walked out without her, he wouldn't come back.

She wasn't ready for that.

But was she ready to jump out of the frying pan and into the fire? This wasn't exactly a picnic Del was planning. He knew the hideouts where Tripp and Holly might go, the people they might turn to when in trouble. And come tomorrow he was going to be there. Looking, asking questions. Stirring up trouble.

"Del." She whispered softly in case he was asleep, in spite of the lack of snoring.

"What?" That nicely deep voice was wide-awake, clear as a bell.

"Tomorrow, what will I do?" She continued to whisper, even though there was no one to hear but Del.

"Get in my way."

She swallowed hard and turned her head to watch the shadow on the other bed. Del filled that bed, long and hard, bigger than she remembered. Not a boy anymore, but a man. A good man. The kind of man every mother dreamed her son would grow up to be. Louise had to be so proud of him.

"I don't want to get in your way, I want to help."

He laughed; it wasn't a pretty sound. "You're not going to help, you're going to get in my way."

"Tripp and Holly, they won't be expecting me. They'll be looking for you, or maybe you and Shock. They won't be looking for a woman." Her heart lurched. She wasn't brave, she wasn't strong—not like this. But those two drug dealers, kidnappers, potential murderers...they wanted her *dead.* She'd do anything to make sure this situation ended as soon as possible and that

Noelle never had the threat of cross fire to worry about. "Maybe together we can catch them off guard."

Del took a long, slow breath. "Tripp's dead."

Vic sat up. "I know you shot him, but he was able to make it out of the cabin...."

"Someone else killed him."

"Someone else," she repeated, her voice low. "Holly?"

"Not likely. We don't know who, we don't know how many." Del didn't sound at all happy about the situation. No wonder he couldn't sleep! "This is not as simple as we originally thought."

Vic rested her head on her hand, propped there on an elbow, and stared at Del's dark shadow. "Will it ever be over?"

"Sure."

"When?"

She was answered with silence, and that dreadful quiet told her more than she needed to know. This could drag on for weeks, months, even. It might never be over.

"I was wrong," she whispered.

"About what?"

He had to know. Was he going to make her say it? Of course he was. "I should have told you about Noelle. Last night, the other afternoon when we were duct-taped to a chair—somewhere in between." A deep breath calmed her. "No, that's not good enough. I should have looked for you years ago." Somewhere in the back of her mind, in that little bit of her youthful self that still believed in fairy tales and pots of gold at the end of the rainbow, she was certain that if Del had known about Noelle, everything would be different. If only he had known...but that was silly. She couldn't go back and undo what had been done.

He didn't say anything, not for a few long minutes. Finally he spoke, his voice as low as hers had been. "She's really…beautiful."

In the dark, Vic smiled. "Of course she is. She looks just like you."

Del's face was lost in shadow, but she did see the shift of his head, and knew that he was trying to look at her, to watch her the way she watched him. In the dimly lit room, he surely couldn't see much. "There's a lot of you in her, too."

"A little."

"More than a little."

Already her heartbeat was slowing, her eyelids were feeling heavy. "She plays softball," Vic said, laying her head on the pillow.

"Really?" He sounded almost excited. He'd been a great baseball player in high school. Vic had been the klutz who couldn't catch a ball to save her life.

"Really."

"Is she any good?"

He seemed so interested. More interested than Preston had ever been. "She's made all-stars every year since she was nine."

"What position?"

"Shortstop."

"We can be pretty sure she got that from me," he said, a lilt of teasing in his soft voice.

Vic pressed her cheek to the pillow. God, she was such an idiot! Preston had never given Noelle the time of day. He'd certainly never shown any pride in Noelle. He'd never said she was beautiful, or asked about her softball games, or made it to a dance recital. Oh, in the beginning he'd tried, for appearances' sake, to be a decent father, but he'd never loved the child he'd agreed to claim as his own. Never. It wasn't right to be un-yielding and cold with a child who tried so hard to gain her father's love and attention.

Del had only known Noelle for a couple of days; he'd only known he was her father for a few hours...and already he'd shown more interest than Preston ever had.

"Do you want to tell her?" Vic whispered. She held her breath as she awaited an answer.

"Do you?" She couldn't help but hear the harshness in that question.

She couldn't make herself get angry all over again. Del should be allowed to be harsh at the moment. "Maybe, when this is all over."

Del took a deep breath. "Maybe."

"I want what's best for her, and for you," Vic admitted. "Who knows? Maybe you two need each other. Maybe when the fireworks settled she'd be good for you and you'd be good for her."

"Fireworks."

"If we decide to tell her, there will most definitely be fireworks."

For a moment Del was silent. Was he reconsidering? "A kid. I swear, Vic, she's almost grown. I missed... everything."

"Not everything." Vic yawned and pulled the covers to her chin. "We still have the boyfriend thing to get through."

Del sat up, straight as a shot. "Boyfriends?"

Vic smiled and closed her eyes. "Boyfriends. She has one, but..."

"You let her have a *boyfriend?*"

"If you can find a way to get past this lovely trade-mark of the teenage years, please let me know."

She heard Del fall back onto the bed. The mattress squeaked loudly as he landed, hard.

"One thing, before you decide whether or not you want to tell Noelle that you're her father," she said as she snuggled beneath the sheets. "If you plan to tell her the news, give her a big hug and then disappear, don't bother. A card at Christmas and the occasional phone call do not a father make. She doesn't need that kind of rejection."

Del was quiet again for a few minutes. He didn't even move around on his bed. "So I'd have to…go to softball games and birthday parties and hang around on occasion just to harass these boyfriends you mentioned."

"Pretty much." He probably wouldn't like the idea at all. It didn't fit with his Jag lifestyle, she was sure. "But don't worry. I can make myself scarce when you come around. I don't expect…" She couldn't help but remember the way he had looked at her when he'd told her not to touch him. The memory of those words cut to the core. And right now, lying in the dark and trying to sort out what was best, she had to admit that he was allowed to be angry. Maybe what she'd done had been unforgivable. "I don't expect anything."

Nothing had been resolved, and still she managed to drift toward sleep.

Louise was in the shower. If Noelle listened close enough, she could hear the water running, even here in the kitchen.

She lifted the receiver and dialed Chris's number. Instead of a ring on the other end she got a tinny recording. His parents had gotten tired of hang-ups at two in the morning, and now had that caller ID that refused to accept phone calls when the numbers had been blocked.

With a huff, Noelle hung up. Why on earth would Louise have her number blocked? Since Michelle's parents had that annoying feature on their phone, she knew exactly which numbers to punch in to disable the function, so her call to Chris would go through.

She dialed again, and the phone rang for ages. Finally, Chris's mother answered. "Hello?"

Noelle thought about hanging up without saying anything. She didn't think Chris's mom liked her much. But thanks to the engaged caller ID she had the number and could always call back. That wouldn't do, especially since Louise was not likely to stay in the shower all day.

"Is Chris there?"

"No, he isn't. Can I take a message?"

A hundred questions crossed Noelle's mind in a flash. Where is he? Who's he with? Has he mentioned me at all since I've been gone? "No," she said. "I'll call back later."

She hung up, listened for the shower again and dialed another number.

Her dad's phone in North Carolina rang four times, before the answering machine picked up. Maybe he was already in Huntsville. When she'd called from the cabin he'd said he had to be there for a few days. Business. When he went to Huntsville it was always for business.

She tried his cell phone, but got that annoying *the customer you are calling is not available* message.

Great. Chris wasn't home and she couldn't get her dad on the phone.

And there was no telling where her mother and that Wilder guy were.

Gross.

Del glanced in the rearview mirror. He hardly recognized himself. The haircut, close shave and removal of his earring had taken care of a good part of the transformation. The khakis and golf shirt were just icing on the cake. He should be able to get close to Kirby Ellis, pool hall owner and small-time crook, without the man having a clue that they'd met before, several weeks ago.

"Don't worry," Vic said. "You look great."

He gave her a quick, sharp glance. "I was checking to see if we were being followed," he said in a low voice.

"Oh. Are we?"

"No."

He gave the road his attention as they neared Birmingham and traffic thickened. "I could drop you off at a friend's…"

"No way," Vic interrupted.

"He's a nice guy, a P.I. here in Birmingham. You and his wife would really hit it off, I'm sure. If you stay with me you're just going to…"

"Get in your way," she interrupted. "Deal with it."

He cast her another cutting glance. "I'll bet whenever Noelle gets stubborn, or does something rash, or butts heads with you, you just stand there and think *She's just like her father.*" He raised his voice an octave in a bad imitation of an irate mother.

Vic fought a smile, and he knew he was right.

"Wrong, baby," he said. "You're more stubborn than I ever was, and this insistence of yours to tag along shows a complete lack of common sense to boot."

She managed to look slightly offended. "I'll have you know I'm a very sensible person."

"Not today, you're not."

She glanced out the window, unable to rationally defend herself. "Why don't you fill me in," she said.

There was a lot she didn't know. "Why did Tripp and Holly come after you in the first place?"

"We're not sure." It was kind of a relief to take his mind off of Vic and turn it to something he had some small control over. "They've been under investigation for a few months. They're small fish in a very big pond, and we're really more interested in the big fish. At this point we're just assuming that they found out I was undercover and decided to…"

"Blow you up," Vic finished when he didn't. "How'd they find me?"

This was where he got befuddled and frustrated. "I don't know. They shouldn't have been able to get that far. All personal information is protected."

"Like your mother."

"Like my mother." A tickle of warning danced up his spine as he glanced at her. How did she manage to look so innocent and beautiful, even now? She hadn't had much sleep since he'd met her; they'd butted heads and argued and almost been killed. And Vic looked as if she'd just stepped out of a magazine ad, all soft and clear-skinned and bright-eyed. She had pulled her curly brown hair back and pinned it up, leaving just a few strands to brush her neck and cheeks. The blue sundress and white sandals she'd bought at the store made her look younger than she was, showing off pale, smooth shoulders and arms and long, well-shaped legs.

This he didn't need. "Maybe they've known I was undercover for a while," he said, trying to turn his mind to the business at hand, "and have been stringing me along while they looked into my background. There's always a way in, if you look hard and long enough." He didn't think Tripp and Holly were that bright, or that patient, but knowing that someone else was behind this operation changed everything.

How the hell had they found Vic? He didn't go undercover using his own name. Which meant that someone had made him and held his cool while he conducted a thorough investigation. The search for personal information would not be easy; it must have taken a long time. He'd traced Del's background, ended up in Huntsville and found Vic. Through someone they'd gone to school with? Someone she'd confided in? There were too damn many questions at this point.

One question niggled at his brain more than the others. What if the man behind this mess was someone who knew him much better than Tripp and Holly ever had or could? Someone who had known right where to look?

"Holly's hurt, so we're going to check out some of the people she hangs with." For all they knew, Holly was as dead as Tripp. She wouldn't have taken her husband's execution-style death well, no matter how badly hurt he'd been. He hoped she wasn't dead. She was all they had.

"Don't they know you?"

"Not well. I met Kirby once, but it was quick and there were several other people around. I'm hoping with the haircut and change of clothes…" He shrugged.

"You do look different." Out of the corner of his eye, he caught a glimpse of her smile. "Why, you're almost respectable."

"Trust me," he said, "it's all an act."

He took his exit, left the interstate too fast and quickly found his way to the downtown street where Holly and Tripp had spent a lot of their time in the past few years. There were two bars they'd frequented, and a rented room over a pool hall.

They were headed for the pool hall. Kirby would know where Holly was, if anyone did.

Del parked on the street and turned to Vic. "Holly has a sister who lives in Tennessee. She mentioned her once, said her name was Cindy and that she was a real stuck-up, pain-in-the-ass, straight-laced do-gooder." He smiled. "For the next half hour or so, you're Cindy. Think you can follow instructions?"

"Of course," she said tightly.

Del shook his head. What the hell was he doing? "Here we go."

Kirby was a small man, a couple of inches taller than Vic and weighing no more than one hundred and thirty pounds. But he was also tough, lean and dead-eyed. Flinty. Vic shivered as she looked at him over the long, empty bar. He was not a nice guy.

It was still too early in the day for the pool hall to be crowded, but Kirby's was open, and three men played at the table in the back of the room, drinking beer and smoking, laughing and casting no more than a single glance at the couple—Vic and Del—who surely did not belong in this rough place.

"I don't know anyone named Holly," the owner of the seedy place said in an emotionless voice.

If she was alone, Vic was certain she'd back out of here without speaking another word. She didn't mind arguing with Del, but this guy? Thankfully Del was behind her to lend emotional as well as substantial support. One of his guns was tucked at his spine beneath a lightweight windbreaker.

"Don't give me that," she said to Kirby, in a tone of voice she normally reserved for Noelle's worst days. "Holly called me, and I could tell by the sound of her voice that something was very, very wrong. We drove down as quickly as we could.''

Kirby laid his black eyes on Del, who had remained quiet to this point. ''Who's he?''

''My...''

''Boyfriend,'' Del said, his voice deep and even. ''Kyle.''

The man behind the bar narrowed one eye as he glared at Cindy. ''I thought you were married,'' he said.

''Well...''

''What she does in her spare time is none of your business,'' Del said impatiently. ''Can we just find this sister and make sure she's okay before we blow the entire day?''

Vic turned to face Del, glad of the opportunity to take her eyes off Kirby for a moment. ''Do you mind?'' she asked testily. ''This is important.''

''Your sister's probably fine,'' he said. ''Let's have a drink or something. She'll call again if she needs anything.''

''She wouldn't have called in the first place if she wasn't in trouble!''

''Look, if she's not here, she's not here.'' He shrugged, seemingly unconcerned. ''We gave it a shot.''

''I'm not satisfied.''

Del gave her a big grin and winked. ''You will be, if we can just get out of here.''

He was playing a role; even his facial expressions were different! He looked so relaxed, so much like the man he was pretending to be. ''Can't you be a little bit patient while I check on my sister?''

''If I *have* to.''

''You're impossible,'' she said softly.

''And you're stubborn as all get-out.''

"Okay, okay," Kirby called.

Vic turned to face Kirby and found him smiling at her. "Holly said you were a real stick-in-the-mud. Guess there are things about you that she doesn't know. You're more like her than I suspected."

Vic gave him her most indignant glare. "My personal life is none of your business, and for your information my sister and I are *nothing* alike."

"Can you just tell her where to find Holly so we can get out of here?" Del asked. "Please?"

Vic gave him a cutting glance. Heaven above, what had she gotten herself into?

Kirby hesitated, but he finally grabbed a matchbook and a pen and scribbled something on the inside cover. "Call this number," he said as he handed the matchbook to Vic. "If Holly wants to see you, she'll tell you where she is."

"Thank you," she said, taking the offered matchbook and being careful not to touch Kirby's fingers. The man was definitely smarmy.

"Yeah, thanks," Del said, taking Vic's arm and almost dragging her toward the door. "You can use my cell to make the call. When she tells you everything is okay, then we can get down to business."

"Forget it, Kyle," she said, sounding more than a little irritable. "I'm not in the mood."

As he opened the door, he slapped her on the butt. "You don't mean that, darlin'."

They stepped onto the cracked sidewalk and the door closed behind them. The windowless pool hall was finally behind them, and Vic sighed in relief. Her knees didn't buckle, but they did go weak.

Del's smile died and he lifted his hand high, two fingers held up in a kind of victory sign.

Vic looked around her but saw nothing. "What are you doing?"

"Giving Shock the high sign. Two fingers means shut down the phone lines so Kirby can't call out."

"What if he has a cell phone?"

Del took her arm and led her toward the car. "By the time he realizes the phone doesn't work and goes for his cell, he will no longer be alone."

Vic saw them approaching then, teams of two from each end of the street. Shock and another man walking toward them from the south, two other men coming from the opposite direction.

"Oh," she said as Del ushered her into the passenger seat. "Aren't you going in with them?"

"Nope," Del said as he slammed her door. When he slipped into the driver's seat and started the engine, he looked directly at her. No more teasing. No more Kyle. "I'm getting you out of here."

As Shock opened the front door to Kirby's, Del pulled the car onto the street.

Vic took a deep breath that calmed her, but not by much. "Why did you claim to be Cindy's boyfriend, *Kyle?* Why not just claim to be the husband? You said this Cindy was a do-gooder, right? Wasn't it risky to claim to be a..." The word *lover* stuck in her throat. "Boyfriend?"

"Embarrassed?"

"Of course not." Being embarrassed was the least of her problems at the moment.

"No rings," Del said.

"What?"

"Neither of us is wearing a wedding ring. Kirby had already checked out our hands. I saw him. He wouldn't have bought the supportive-husband bit."

"Oh. I didn't notice him checking out our hands."

"Yep."

"So if you'd said we were married, he would have known we were lying, and..."

"And people would be shooting at us again."

She was going to have to learn to trust Del, at least where his job was concerned. Trust wasn't something she found easily these days. "Now what?"

"Now nothing. Your part here is done. Shock will call when they get out of Kirby's, we give him the phone number Kirby gave you and then we wait."

"Wouldn't you rather be—" her heart hitched and her mouth went dry "—helping Shock?"

"Yes," he said without hesitation.

When Del's cell phone rang, she almost jumped out of her seat. When he reached out his hand for the matchbook, she handed it to him, placing the closed matchbook on that offered palm.

He was right—she would only get in the way. She wasn't cut out for this.

Del's conversation with Shock was short and to the point. When he ended the call and placed the cell phone on the console, Vic took a deep breath. For courage.

"Maybe you were right last night."

"I'm sure I was. About what?"

"Me getting in the way."

He glanced at her, all too briefly. "You did fine."

"Yeah, but...there's no reason why you can't find a place to stash me for a few days. You mentioned a friend. Someone I could stay with?"

"No," he answered, low and short.

"But you said..."

"That just would've been for a few hours. I dragged you into this, Vic. I'm not leaving you until it's over."

That declaration should have terrified her, but instead she was uncommonly relieved.

Chapter 9

Vic didn't ask where they were going. She probably expected another cheap motel, something miles off the interstate. A ratty hideaway. Something dim and uninviting. But she didn't ask, and she didn't complain.

Maybe she didn't ask because she thought silence was best. There was too much unfinished between them, good and bad. She stared out the window, at mile after mile where the scenery didn't change. Where was her mind?

When he was able to think rationally, he knew he shouldn't blame her for doing whatever she needed to in order to protect Noelle. In fact, he should thank her, even now, when Vic's idea of protecting the kid was to keep Noelle away from her own father and the danger and heartbreak he might bring. He should be able to understand that, rationally.

But when he looked at Vic, he didn't always think

rationally. He thought with his gut, the emotions he usually controlled without so much as a hitch.

Even if he could convince himself that she did have her reasons for not telling him about Noelle now, when she was afraid criminals like Tripp and Holly might find and use that information, he couldn't make himself forgive her for not telling him about the baby all those years ago. She could have looked for him when she found out she was pregnant. She could have *told* him that he was going to be a father, even if the idea of making him a part of her life was repugnant and unthinkable.

A father. The very idea made him shudder. He hadn't known his own father, and none of the men his mother took in from time to time had ever been what anyone would call a fitting father figure. When she'd met Eugene Kelsey, a good man who'd loved her the way she deserved to be loved, Del had been grown and long past needing a man to play daddy.

But what about Noelle? Did she need him now? Or was she long past needing a father?

No. He'd heard the need in Noelle's voice when she'd called Preston. It wasn't too late.

They'd been driving for an hour and a half, and Vic had been completely quiet for the past hour. Just as well. Had she so much as turned her eyes his way? Probably not. But suddenly she seemed to realize where they were heading.

She turned her head slowly. "Are you taking me home?"

"Yep."

Home should be safe, it should be a haven. Tripp and Holly had robbed Vic of that security. She paled a little, her hands clenched into tiny fists.

"Is it safe?"

"Shock had the place checked thoroughly late last night, and someone has been watching the place since then. Nothing going on there. It's all clear." He caught and held her wide-eyed stare. "We won't stay there long. I have some things in the Jag I want to get, and I'm sure you'd like to pack a bag of your own stuff."

"Yeah," she whispered.

"If the lab team is finished at the cabin, Shock should be able to drop off the things we left behind while we're there. If not tonight, tomorrow morning, for sure."

"Noelle's things, too, I imagine," she said softly.

"Yeah. Maybe I can get Shock to make a run out to my mom's, drop off Noelle's things and check on the two of them."

Vic nodded.

Noelle was a delicate subject at the moment. Time to move on. "We should know soon if they managed to round up Holly." He'd feel better once that was done, even though he now knew she was not working alone. Without Tripp, Holly was bound to be unpredictable. Tripp had never been overly bright, but he had always been steadier than Holly. He was the one who kept her from flying off the handle, from acting irrationally and then regretting it later. Yeah, without Tripp, Holly was a much more dangerous opponent.

When they pulled onto Vic's street, Del spotted the car that had been posted at the curb as lookout, and lifted his hand to signal the local cop who sat in the driver's seat. The guy looked bored. Of course he was bored. Stakeout was the most tedious duty imaginable, and this wasn't even a local case. Shock had called in a few favors to get this kind of cooperation.

Del escorted Vic into the house, looked over the place

upstairs and down, then left her in the kitchen while he went to talk to the cop at the curb.

"Anything?" Del asked as he approached the car.

"Not even a Girl Scout or a Jehovah's Witness to break the monotony," the cop said with a yawn.

"Del Wilder, DEA." Del offered his hand as the cop left his car.

"John Bohannon, HPD, burglary."

They shook hands, each commented on the tedium of a stakeout, then Del dismissed the investigator with his thanks. As Bohannon drove away, Del headed back for the house. He and Vic would be in and out, an hour at the most, and they wouldn't be back until this was over. There was no need for a continuing stakeout.

His cell phone rang as he reached the porch.

"Wilder," he said as he entered the house and closed the door behind him.

"She's gone," Shock said sharply. "We didn't miss her by any more than half an hour, I swear."

"She knew you were coming?"

"Maybe. Maybe not. We got to Kirby before he could've made the call, but there were other people around, three guys playing pool. Someone might have realized what was going on and warned her, but I don't think so. We had the place locked down quick, and I didn't find a cell phone on any of the pool players. I think it was just bad luck."

"Bad luck?"

"It's been a bad week, man. Let's face it. We ain't got the ol' mojo on this case."

That was putting it mildly. "What did you find at her place?"

"She's hurt and trying to doctor herself. Judging by

the amount of blood we found in the room where she was hiding out, she's hurt pretty bad.''

One wild shot in the dark as he'd rolled off the porch and still he'd hit her. Too bad Holly hadn't gone down then and there.

"Where are you?" Shock asked.

"Vic's."

"Get out of there, man. Now. Holly knows that place. If she's mad enough and not thinking straight, that might be where she's headed. If she's mobile, she's headed your way."

"Give me five minutes and we're out of here," Del said. "I'll call you later." With that he disconnected, swore beneath his breath and headed for the kitchen. All was quiet here, there was no sign of Vic. He went back the way he had come and climbed the stairs, taking them two at a time.

"Vic!" he called. "Let's go!" Her bedroom door stood open, and he stopped there in the doorway. She sat on the edge of the bed, head down, suitcase sitting open on the bed, empty. "Hurry up," he said, his voice lower and calmer. "They didn't get Holly. We've got to get out of here now."

Vic lifted her head and laid her eyes on him, fearless, determined. "No," she said softly.

"No?" Del stepped inside the room. "The odds are, Holly will come here first thing, looking for you. Let's go." He reached out and took her arm.

"Maybe we should let her come," Vic said, her voice remaining calm. She tilted her head back to look him in the eye. "This might never be over, if we keep running and she keeps chasing and…and I want it to be over."

Of course she did. When this was over, she could send him away. "Vic, that's not smart." He tried to reason with her, but from the strangely serene expression on her face, none of it sunk in. God, the woman was stubborn!

"With Noelle out of the house and safe, maybe we should think about just—" she took a deep breath and exhaled slowly "—staying here. Waiting. This cat-and-mouse thing could go on forever, and…" She went pale, her already colorless face going almost white. "We need to end this once and for all. Noelle won't be safe as long as Holly is out there. I can't live with that."

"You're talking about making yourself bait, Vic," Del said sharply. "Do you really want to sit here and wait for Holly and God knows who else to show up and try to kill us again?"

"Yes," she answered calmly.

He went for her weak spot. "If something happens to you, who'll take care of Noelle?"

She lifted her eyes and laid them on him, too soft, too sweet. "First of all, I do trust you to make sure that nothing happens to me."

"I can only do so much." He had no idea how they might be attacked. When. With what kind of force.

"What about you?" she whispered. "You say you want to be a father, that you want Noelle to know about you. If anything happens to me, you might get your chance."

Didn't she know better? Didn't she know what he would do to protect her? "Baby, if Holly gets to you that means I'm already dead."

"If anything happens…" Vic began.

"Let's cut the 'if anything happens' crap. Say it like it is, Vic. What we're talking about is you ending up *dead*."

"I know," she whispered.

"Say it," he said, certain she didn't grasp the severity of the situation.

"I could end up dead," she said, her voice soft but not at all shaky. "But I don't think that will happen." For a split second, she looked as if she was going to reach out and touch him. And then she didn't. "I think you're very good at what you do, Del. You can keep me safe."

"Vic, you haven't thought this through."

"I have. For the past few hours, I haven't thought about anything else."

Del gave up and sat on the side of the bed, a couple of feet away from Vic. "It'll be dangerous."

"I imagine so."

In the end, he was the one to reach out and touch her, brushing back a curling length of honey-colored hair. He couldn't stay angry with her, no matter what she'd done. She was the mother of his daughter and she'd done everything in her power to protect the child. Part of that protection was from him, which still rankled, but he did owe her…something.

"I'll make the arrangements."

The living-room drapes were closed tight, and Del paced nervously while Vic perched on the couch. He had finally agreed to stay here, but he didn't really like the idea. Surely he knew she was right. It was best to get this over with, once and for all.

Shock and four other agents were watching the house from all angles, but it was Del's presence that made her feel safe.

It was nice to be home, no matter what the circumstances. She was more comfortable in her own clothes— loose-fitting blue pants and a matching top that were cool and comfortable. She should use the opportunity to paint, but she'd left many of her supplies at the cabin, when they'd escaped in the night. She had brushes and paints here, though, as well as a number of blank canvases, but she knew she'd never be able to make her mind be still enough to work, not with Del in the house and Holly on the loose.

No, instead of painting today she'd wandered the house aimlessly, searched for answers...and now she sat on the couch clasping her hands and watching Del pace.

They still hadn't come to any decision regarding Noelle. Should they tell her Del was her father? Wait a while? Keep it a secret forever? She wished there was an easy answer, a way to take back the hurt Del felt and still keep Noelle safe. She hadn't been able to come up with that answer, or anything close.

She jumped when the doorbell rang, something deep inside her remembering the morning she'd been kidnapped, when she'd walked to the door blithely unaware of the events that would follow. Del grabbed a walkie-talkie from his belt and flicked a switch.

"Go ahead."

Shock's tinny voice answered. "Female, dark hair, approximately five foot six. Really nice hooters."

Vic rolled her eyes.

"She's alone," Shock continued. "Got here in a red minivan."

Vic relaxed. "That's Wanda," she said. "My friend. She's okay."

Del relayed the message, and Vic went to answer the door just as Wanda rung the bell for the second time.

"Where have you been?" Wanda asked as she stepped into the foyer.

Vic glanced around. There was no sign of the surveillance she knew the house was under. No suspicious vans, no shaking bushes. Five men were watching. Where *were* they?

"I've been worried sick."

"I'm sorry," Vic said as she followed Wanda to the kitchen. "I should have called…"

Wanda came up short as she entered the kitchen, then turned to Vic and smiled wickedly. "You're forgiven," she said softly. "Wow."

Vic followed Wanda into the kitchen and saw the reason for her friend's smile. Del stood at the counter, his back to them, making coffee and looking very much at home.

"Hi," Wanda said, walking straight toward Del, who turned at the sound of her greeting. "I'm Wanda Freeman."

"Del Wilder." He offered his hand for a shake as Wanda came near. "I've heard a lot about you."

Not a *lot,* Vic thought as she watched the two shake hands. She'd told Del that Wanda was her friend, and that they'd learned the single-mother routine together— since Wanda's husband had passed away just months after Vic's divorce. She hadn't told him that having Wanda around had kept her sane for the past six years. That confession would be far too telling.

"That's just not fair," Wanda said, her smile widening. "I haven't heard a *thing* about you."

"Vic and I are old friends."

Wanda accepted that explanation, nodding her head. And then her eyes lit up. "Del! Are you the guy Vic's dad—"

"No," Vic said sharply. "Del, Wanda and I are going to sit in the living room. Let me know when the coffee is ready." With that, she took Wanda by the elbow and led her from the kitchen. When had she mentioned Del to Wanda? She didn't remember ever saying anything. Not a word!

And then it hit her. There had been that one night, four or five years ago, where they'd finished off a bottle of wine and spilled their guts to each other. It had been one of those really bad Valentine's Days, and they'd decided to declare it a man-free holiday and celebrate their singleness together. The night was a hazy memory, and had been the very next morning. How much had she said? Surely she hadn't told Wanda that Del was Noelle's father. Surely not.

Too bad Wanda's memory was so much better than her own.

"He's so cute," Wanda said softly as they reached the living room. "No, not cute, that's the wrong word. He's more like…gorgeous. Wow."

Vic couldn't make herself return Wanda's smile. Not only did Wanda know too much, she wasn't safe here. How could she kick her friend out without explaining everything? Wanda wasn't one to run from a fight. If she knew there was trouble, she'd insist on helping. That would never do. "Del doesn't know about what my dad did," Vic whispered, "and I'd just as soon not tell him."

"Why not?" Wanda's own smile disappeared. "That happened ages ago. What difference does it make—"

"I would just rather not go there," Vic said too sharply.

"Okay," Wanda said, unhappy with the decision but agreeable.

As much as she would like to curl up on the couch with Wanda and watch old movies and talk about the kids—her Noelle and Wanda's three boys—it was too risky. What if Wanda was here when Holly dropped by?

Vic shuddered. Too many people she loved were in danger.

"This is really not a good time," she said, her voice low.

"I can see that." Wanda waggled her eyebrows.

"No, not..." Oh hell, what difference did it make what Wanda thought? All that mattered was getting her out of here before anything happened. "You know how it is."

"I wish!" Wanda's easy grin came back. "I haven't had a decent date in months, and I can't remember the last time I had a good-looking man in the kitchen making coffee."

When the doorbell rang, Vic jumped out of her skin again. Del headed for the front door, casting a glance her way as he passed. A moment later, Del led Shock into the living room.

"Vic," Del said. "You remember my friend Albert."

"Sure."

The agitated man cast a warning glare at Del. "Shock," he said, offering his hand to Wanda. "Albert Shockley's the name, but everyone calls me Shock."

"Wanda. Wanda Freeman."

The two shook hands, and when Wanda turned around to face Vic, her back to both men, she mouthed that word again. *Wow.* A wow for Shock? She didn't get it. Over Wanda's shoulder, Shock was mouthing something at Del. From the expression on his face, his excitement had nothing to do with Holly, surveillance, or any other kind of official business. He was probably all excited about Wanda's *hooters.* Men.

The four of them had a quick cup of coffee, and Shock and Wanda talked about music. Stevie Ray Vaughan and

Miles Davis, specifically. They were each delighted to find someone of a like mind where music was concerned.

Del contributed nothing to the conversation. He was wound tighter than usual; in fact, he was downright jumpy. Every now and then he looked as if he really wanted to physically toss Shock and Wanda out of the house.

Vic couldn't seem to make her mind settle down long enough to absorb much of anything that was said, so she just settled back and watched. She watched Wanda and Shock charm each other, and she watched Del brood.

Maybe he hadn't been paying attention to the segment of the sentence Wanda had spoken before being interrupted and led from the kitchen. She could hope for that, right? She could really, really hope that his mind had been elsewhere at that moment or his hearing had failed him. So much had happened lately…that surely wasn't too much to ask.

To say Wanda and Shock hit it off would be an understatement. Wanda was immediately smitten with the gangly man with the quick smile, and it was obvious that Shock was attracted to Wanda.

Wanda saw that attraction, too; she was no dummy where men were concerned. They weren't far into their conversation when she gave Shock "the ultimate test" and mentioned her three boys. The widow had been burned before, by men who were attracted to her good looks and her easy laugh but then backed off when they found out she had three kids under the age of ten.

Shock didn't seem at all taken aback by the news; he didn't even blink. He actually asked questions about the boys.

Del didn't say much, but every now and then Vic caught him staring at her. Too hard. She wanted Wanda out of here and safe, but she dreaded the moment she and Del were alone once again. Nothing had been settled between them. Would it ever be?

Shock suggested that the four of them take in a movie. Del quickly declined, in a smooth way that told Vic this had all been planned via two-way radio. Wanda didn't seem to mind when Shock mentioned that the two of them could go on alone, and she quickly agreed, since her mother had the boys for the evening. That had been the plan all along, Vic imagined, to get Wanda out of the house. Shock wasn't the only man on guard duty—there were two DEA agents, as well as two local detectives, watching the house and waiting for Holly to make her appearance. Apparently they could afford to lose Shock for a couple of hours.

Shock and Wanda said their goodbyes, and as they left Del locked the door behind them. He stood there for a moment, his hand on the dead bolt, then he turned to face her.

His dark blue eyes had gone deep, unreadable. Tension was evident in the set of his jaw, the twitch of his mouth. Moving slowly, with deliberation, he crossed his arms over his chest.

She could run, she supposed, but there was no place to hide.

Finally Del spoke. "Am I the guy your dad...would you care to finish that sentence for me?"

"Not really," Vic answered softly.

"He didn't even know about us, did he?"

They had gone to great pains to make sure that he didn't know. Vic had known all along that Del Wilder, with his long hair, bartender mother and sinful charm, was not the kind of guy her father would approve of.

Knowing that didn't make her love him any more, or any less.

Del had only come by the house when her father was gone. They met on the sly and tried to hide how they felt from everyone. And it hadn't been enough.

"He found out," she whispered.

"So? What did he *do*, Vic?"

Maybe Wanda was right. This had happened ages ago. It wasn't important. It was ancient history, bad memories she'd managed to put behind her a long time ago. So why didn't she want to tell Del what had happened? Because she was afraid she'd break down and cry, and she didn't want him to know her weakness? Because it was too late to change what had happened?

Or because, deep in her heart, she still blamed Del. Just a little.

"He threatened to have you arrested for statutory rape," she said, trying to keep her voice steady.

"What?" It was clear from the expression on his face, this was not what Del had expected to hear.

"You'd had your eighteenth birthday," she said. "I hadn't."

"Yeah, but...he didn't have me arrested."

Vic shook her head. "Because I did as he asked." What difference did it make? After all this time...no difference at all. So why did tears sting her eyes? "I sent you away." She'd stood on the porch—hands clasped too tight, heart beating too hard—knowing her father was behind the door listening closely, knowing she had no choice but to do as he commanded. There hadn't been a chance to warn Del that she didn't mean what she said, no way to get a message to him to stay away from the house.

She'd been terrified that night: of her father, of losing

Del, of the horrible feeling of helplessness that churned inside her. She'd known what her father was doing was wrong, but she didn't know how to get around his demands and his threats. She didn't know how to save Del from her father and keep him at the same time, and every emotion had bubbled wildly inside her. Fear. Love. Anger.

Vic felt that way now, her stomach churning, her eyes burning. "I sent you away." She looked up at Del, her eyes accusing, her heart breaking, after all this time. "And you *left*."

Chapter 10

Del felt like someone had just kicked him in the gut; it was becoming a familiar feeling.

"What?"

He expected Vic to tell him to forget it, to turn her back on him and stalk away, but she didn't. She hit him in the chest with the flat of her hand. Hard. "You just *left*," she said, still sounding stunned. Sounding amazed and hurt and betrayed. She dropped her eyes, likely so he couldn't see the tears that sprung there, but the move came too late. "You believed me," she said softly, hitting him again. Since there wasn't any real anger or power in that blow, he ignored it. "I told you that I didn't love you, that I didn't want to see you anymore...but you should have known better. You should have..."

A tear slipped down her cheek and she turned her back on him and walked away. Again, the move came too late to hide her response.

"Vic..." he called as he followed her.

"Forget it," she snapped. "That was a long time ago. A lifetime ago. I'm just upset by everything that's happened recently. It has nothing to do with something that happened a hundred years ago. I'm not used to people trying to blow me up or shoot me. It might be an everyday occurrence to you, but I find it quite upsetting."

"Look at me."

She didn't. Instead she ran up the stairs. "Good night," she said, trying to sound calm and falling far short. Del stood at the foot of the stairs and listened as Vic ran to her room and closed the door.

He wandered purposefully through the bottom floor of the house, checking the locks on the front and back doors, double-checking the latches on the windows, using the walkie-talkie to check with the agent who was now in charge until Shock returned. And all the time his mind was only half on the tasks at hand. The other half was caught up in that really bad, warm night, sixteen years ago.

He should've known Vic hadn't meant the things she'd said. He'd thought her agitation and the tears that had been so quick to spring to her eyes had been caused by nervousness, not fear. And it had been so easy for him to believe that he was nothing more than a diversion for the little rich girl, the boy from the wrong side of the tracks who had been fun for a while. Nothing more. Everything between them had happened so fast, he'd had his very breath stolen away. His breath and his young heart and his reason. He'd felt like such a chump, for loving her. So he'd walked away without looking back, never imagining, never wondering...

Del climbed the stairs slowly, his feet like lead, his heart the same. He'd hated Vic for dumping him that way, he'd cursed her for years for being so cold. And all that time she'd been protecting him. No one had ever protected him before, not like that. *He'd* taken care of his mother, fellow soldiers in the marines, his partners in his years with the DEA…even the women who had been a part of his life in the past sixteen years. He was the strong one, right? No trembling, scared little girl could possibly protect him.

But Vic had. And if Wanda hadn't let something slip tonight, he never would have known. He might have walked away again, when this was over, without knowing what had happened.

In the upstairs hallway, he stopped before Vic's closed door. He laid his hand on the doorknob. If it was locked, he'd move on. If she'd locked him out, he'd let her be. He was considering not turning that knob, locked or not, when he heard a soft sob.

The door opened easily, and he stepped inside. Vic lay on her still-made bed, her back to him, her body curled up and rigid. Only the soft shaking of her shoulders and the occasional sniffle gave her away. She didn't turn to face him, and she didn't tell him to get out. She just lay there, fighting tears. Angry, after all this time, that he had believed her when she'd told him she didn't want to see him again. Ever.

He laid his walkie-talkie on the bedside table, and removed the Glock from his waistband. When he placed the pistol on the table beside the radio, it landed with a thud that was too loud in the quiet room. Vic jumped a little, but she didn't roll over to face him and she didn't order him from the room.

Del sat on the side of the bed, knowing that he couldn't leave Vic this way. Moving slowly, he lay down on his side, draped his arm around Vic's waist and pulled her back against his chest. She didn't fight, but instead melted into him gratefully, even as she choked back the tears.

"I'm sorry," he whispered, holding her tight.

Vic shook her head. "Don't be." Sobs shook her voice, but she tried to sound calm, collected as always. "I don't know why I got so upset. It's just…everything else getting to me, I suppose."

"It was a long time ago," Del said softly.

Vic nodded.

"So why do I sometimes feel like it happened yesterday?" Over the years, he'd told himself that the pain of that final encounter was so sharp only because it had been his first brush with heartache. Only brush with heartache, to be honest. No other woman had ever worked her way into his heart the way Vic had, the way she still did. Dammit.

"I was so *angry*," she admitted. "With my father, of course, but also with you. I loved you. You should have known I wouldn't just…" She took a deep breath, to stop more tears, he imagined. "I kept waiting for you to come back," she whispered. "I convinced myself that you surely knew I didn't mean anything I'd said. As soon as it was safe, you'd come to my window at midnight and…and rescue me. You didn't, and I never forgave you for that."

He ran his fingers through her curling hair. "You never came back to school."

"There were just a couple of weeks left, and my father told my teachers I was sick. I finished up at home and got my diploma in the mail. My father had me watched…." She made a sound somewhere between a laugh and a sob. "That's how he knew about us. He began to suspect there was something going on and he hired a detective to follow me.''

''Bastard,'' Del muttered.

''I wanted to sneak out of the house and go to you,'' Vic continued, ''but I was afraid he'd carry out his threat if I got caught. No, I *knew* he would. He had the connections to make it stick no matter what I said, and I couldn't bear the idea of you going to jail. I couldn't bear the idea of you going to jail because…because you loved me.''

''And when you found out about the baby?'' Del whispered.

''You were gone. Your mother was gone. And I was left with no one to turn to but my father, the man who'd driven you away. The man who'd forced *me* to drive you away.'' Impossibly, she snuggled tighter against him. She was warm and soft and real, and he loved the feel of her here, in his arms.

''He tried to make me…get rid of the baby, but I refused. And there are some things even my father couldn't force. He did try, but I told the doctor I wanted to have my baby, and that was the end of that.'' She sniffled. ''So good old Dad arranged a marriage with Preston. Otherwise I would have ended up on the street with nothing, and believe me, that was another threat he would have carried out.'' She turned her face down. ''I even looked for you at the wedding, glancing over my shoulder as I walked down the aisle, hesitating with my vows…I was so sure that if I stalled long enough you would be there. You didn't come. I hated you then,'' she said softly, her voice muffled by the pillow. ''For not being there, for believing me when I said I didn't love you. You should have known….''

''Yes, I should have.''

"You should have been there."

"I know. I wish I had been." No wonder Vic didn't trust him! Her father had betrayed her, Preston had betrayed her, and he…he'd left when she needed him most. "I'm here now."

"Too late," she whispered.

"Is it?"

Vic didn't answer but snuggled closer to him, put her hand over one of his and took a deep breath. They lay there that way for a long time, it seemed, before her breathing became deep and even and he knew she was asleep. Good. She needed her rest. The past several days had been tough, emotionally and physically.

She needed her rest, and he needed to hold her.

Vic opened her eyes to soft moonlight and the comforting feel of Del's arms around her. The deep, even rise and fall of the chest that was pressed against her spine told her he was sleeping.

She hadn't planned or wanted to tell him what had happened all those years ago. It didn't matter now, she kept telling herself. Water under the bridge, old news, unimportant, ancient…so why did it sometimes seem, like he'd said, that it had happened yesterday?

The girl she had been and the woman she had become were so very different, she knew if her father gave her that ultimatum today, she'd fight. Back then, she hadn't known how to fight, or even that she could. Now…she had become a fighter, hadn't she? No one pushed her around anymore. She didn't take any man's advice or direction. It had been a long time coming, but she was her own woman, and it was nice.

It was also a little lonely, she decided, though it hadn't

seemed so until Del showed up, reminding her of everything she'd missed.

Moving carefully, she twisted in Del's arms until she faced him. Her nose touched his chest, one leg slipped between his and she draped an arm around his waist. His answer was to pull her more tightly against his warm body. After all this time, did she love him still? Or was this feeling she couldn't shake nothing more than an echo of a memory?

Vic tried to tell herself that what she felt was merely physical, but that in itself was amazing. She wasn't a physical person. She didn't get turned on, she didn't…she didn't throb this way when a man touched her. In the years since Del had walked away…in the years since she'd *sent* him away…she hadn't craved the touch of any man the way she craved Del now. She hadn't wanted to lose herself in a man's touch, in passion and a need so great it had the power to consume.

She slipped her fingers beneath his T-shirt, yearning for the feel of his skin against her hand. He was harder now than he'd been then, tougher and rougher. But his skin was smooth, warm and enticing. She loved it, the sensation of his skin against her hand.

She wasn't sure when he came awake, but he did. His hand copied hers, slipping beneath her blouse, touching gently. Her skin tingled, her entire body responded to a touch so simple.

Del flicked open the buttons of her blouse, moving languidly, accomplishing the task easily. Vic answered by slipping both hands beneath his T-shirt and holding on to him with her palms steady and her fingers rocking.

When the blouse was completely unbuttoned, Del opened it slowly, peeling back the fabric as he rolled her onto her back. He kissed her, first on the mouth, then on the throat, his mouth finally trailing down to the valley between her breasts. His fingers worked the clasp, and when the bra was gone, tossed onto the floor along with the blouse, Del raked his fingers across her nipples. They pebbled at his touch, and when he laid his mouth on her there, she closed her eyes and lost herself. She hadn't lost herself in such a long time, and he made it easy. So very easy.

Her body screamed for his, but he took his time. He suckled and caressed her breasts, he touched her gently, and when he rose up and laid his mouth over hers, she kissed him greedily, wrapping her arms around his neck and holding on tight while their tongues danced and their bodies aligned.

She reached between their bodies and touched him, raking her palm over his denim-covered erection. He moaned as she traced her fingers over his length, testing and teasing, amazed and aroused. She unbuckled his jeans and lowered the zipper, her hand shaking as she accomplished the task.

Del filled her hand, hot and hard, and she caressed him again. He moaned this time, and she caught the moan in her mouth, tasting it, cherishing it.

Her own trousers, a soft cotton more cooperative than his blue jeans, were whisked down and off, and she was laid completely bare beneath him.

She didn't believe in much anymore, she didn't willingly place herself in anyone's hands. But this…she felt herself giving more and more of herself to Del. More than her body, more than her closely guarded trust. She slipped her hands beneath his waistband and pushed his jeans down, her hands caressing his bare backside as she halfway undressed him, her body wrapping around his. A leg over his, an arm around his neck.

He touched her intimately, his fingers dancing over her wet flesh. She throbbed all the more, arched her back to bring him closer, and her breath caught low in her throat. He found the sensitive nub at her entrance and circled his fingertip there, until she was sure she could wait no longer, until she was ready to scream and come off the bed.

And then he was there, slowly pressing himself against her, and then inside her, easing the pain of need and ending the aching sensation of being hollow without him. He completed her, filling her slowly, again taking his time.

Her own anxiousness faded, now that he was inside her. She was on the edge of climax, but she didn't want this to end. Not yet. She wanted his body against hers, deep inside hers, a part of hers. She wanted this sensation of being one to go on and on. Her heart beat too fast, she couldn't breathe, completion teased her with ribbons of pleasure that fluttered through her body.

He began to move, rhythmically, slowly. He would almost leave her, and then with a steady thrust he filled her again. Every sensation was intense, new, more wonderful than she had imagined or remembered. The air was clearer, sharper, and nothing else mattered but this—the way they felt when they came together. He was beautiful, the way he touched her was heavenly, and each long, slow thrust was more extraordinary than the last. She rocked against Del, drew him deep, held him there. And shattered.

It was unlike anything she had experienced or expected. The waves of pleasure were intense, incredible...and as she felt Del come with her, she cried out loud and held on tight.

The words *I love you* were on her lips, but she bit

them back. This wasn't love, it was just a persistent physical attraction she couldn't—wouldn't—fight anymore. Not tonight, anyway.

She ran the tips of her fingers through Del's short hair, marveling at the feel of the silky strands.

"Stay with me tonight," she whispered.

"I'm here."

"All night."

"I'm not going anywhere."

"Take this off," she said, smiling as she tugged on his T-shirt. "And this." She ran a hand down his hip to the waistband of his jeans. "And…" *Hold me tight and don't let go.* She couldn't say that. It sounded too desperate. Too needy. "And kiss me again." She drew his mouth to hers, still hungry for that touch. Could she ever get enough of this?

"I'm so tired of fighting with you," she said, her lips still brushing his, her fingers playing with his black-as-night hair. "For tonight, let's not argue."

"Another truce?" he teased.

"A cease-fire," she said with a smile.

"We'll just hunker down in the foxhole for the night."

"All's quiet on the Southern front."

"I surrender."

Vic pulled Del's mouth to hers once again. "Me, too."

They did sleep, but it would be a lie to say they passed a restful night. All barriers were down, and surrender turned out to be very, very nice. They'd touched, and talked and made love for a second time. They caressed each other like old lovers who'd been apart for a long time and were relearning old curves and lines and finding new ones.

He'd checked in with the detail surrounding the house more than once. Shock had long been back from his movie date with Wanda, and if Del didn't know better, he'd say his friend and partner was well on his way to being infatuated. Shock was a wonder with women, but he didn't get emotionally involved. His work was too important, and the idea of being tied down to one place and one woman was too much for him to bear. But he certainly had enjoyed his evening with Wanda Freeman, more than usual.

All was quiet, where the surveillance of Vic's house was concerned. In a way that was good, but…if anything was going to happen, it needed to happen quickly. There was no way the powers-that-be would continue to okay the expense of this detail if it didn't pan out in a few days.

Del forgot the reason he was here, he forgot that the house was surrounded by a detail made up of local cops and DEA agents, and just watched the woman beside him. She slept again, on her stomach this time, her face buried in a soft pillow, her bare back pale and shapely in the moonlight cast through the window, the white sheet barely covering her nicely rounded bottom.

Vic had always been beautiful. As a girl, as a woman, as the mother of his child. As a lover, she was striking. Giving, demanding and peaceful, all at the same time. Moonlight made her skin look pale, her hair silver, the hands that had reached for him through the night, fragile. He loved her hands. Talented, strong, gentle as a spring breeze.

Del took the sheet that covered Vic between two fingers and slowly pulled it down, gradually baring her backside and thighs and calves for him. She was so beautiful, the sight of her lying there took his breath away. Literally. Completely.

Moving slowly, he leaned over and down and kissed the backs of her knees, one at a time. She sighed but didn't move. His hands skimmed up the backs of her thighs and over her backside, the sight of his clumsy-looking hands against her delicate skin fascinating. He kissed her again, at the base of her spine this time, and again she sighed. Her fingers moved, then, rocking against the sheet. She turned her head. And as he worked his mouth up her spine, she came fully awake. He felt it first, in the way she breathed and in the way her body moved beneath his mouth. He heard it, in the sigh that was not one mindlessly uttered in sleep. And he saw it, when his leisurely trip up Vic's back ended at her neck and she opened her eyes. And smiled.

She didn't smile enough these days. At least, she hadn't since his return. He wanted to see her smile more often, he wanted to make her laugh. He wanted to see just a hint of the carefree girl he'd loved in the woman he craved to distraction.

She rolled over beneath him, circling her arms around his neck as she came to rest on her back. Her eyes were sleepily hooded but smiling, her lips were full and inviting. He kissed those lips, unable not to, and as he kissed her, Vic wrapped her legs around his. Her fingers caressed his erection as she guided him to her.

He surged forward to fill her, burying himself in her wet heat. Her body caressed his, welcomed his, and once again he forgot everything but the way she felt when she was so completely wrapped around him. He'd never known anything as powerful as the way they made love. He told himself it was the intensity of the past week that made the way they came together so potent. It was their past, intruding, or some freak chemical attraction…and then he quit reasoning and just loved her.

He pushed deep, and Vic arched up off the bed and threw her head back. She climaxed with a throaty cry that stole the last of his resolve. The release was as powerful as he had known it would be, as complete and earth-shattering as the first time he'd made love to her tonight. And the second. He had a terrible feeling, as he laid his head on her shoulder and breathed deep, that he would never get enough of her. Never.

Vic cradled his head and hooked her leg more firmly around his. "I love you," she whispered sleepily, and then she drifted off once again, while he was still inside her, while their hearts still beat too fast and the blood flowed through their veins too furiously.

He wondered if Vic would remember what she'd said, come morning, or if she thought this was all part of a dream. And who was she speaking to? The Del who lay with her now? Or the Del she'd loved as a girl? He didn't want to be nothing more than a fond memory, the faint but undeniable allure of a first love. He wanted…hell, he didn't know what he wanted.

His suitcase, in Noelle's room where he'd expected to be sleeping tonight, contained a pack of condoms. He hadn't made a trip to that room tonight, and Vic hadn't suggested that he should. Maybe this was the wrong time of the month for her to get pregnant, though even he knew that was a poor excuse for birth control. Maybe she'd been so caught up in sensation she'd forgotten.

He was normally so careful. He didn't have unprotected sex, ever. But something primal, something basic and deep and undeniable, wanted to see and experience everything he'd missed last time. He wanted to watch

Vic grow. He wanted to lay his hand over her rounded belly, listen to the heartbeat of a growing child, talk to the baby as it grew, day by day. He had no right to want these things, he knew, but in the night, in the dark, with a naked Vic sleeping beneath him, it seemed like a fine idea.

Chapter 11

Vic woke when the sun touched her eyelids, the bothersome light intruding on a dream. She could tell, as her eyes fluttered open, that it was well into the morning. She never slept this late!

Rolling over languidly, she ran smack-dab into the reason for her uncustomary sleeping habits. Del was sprawled there with the sheet to his waist, his back to her. He was naked, of course, and sleeping deeply. And he was so tempting he tugged at her heart, even now.

When she'd thought of him over the years, more often than she'd liked or admitted, she always remembered his long hair. She'd loved it, years ago, so thick and silky. But she liked it short, she decided. It suited the new Del, who was a harder, fiercer man than the boy she'd once loved had been. The long hair had softened the distinct line of his jaw, the power in his neck, the strength of his shoulders.

Vic left the bed gingerly, trying not to wake Del.

Maybe she could be bold in the dark, but by the light of day she would be more cautious. She wasn't fearless, not by any means, she thought as she grabbed her robe from the closet and slipped it on. She really should head downstairs, make some coffee, maybe make Del breakfast.

But she wasn't through looking at Del. She turned around, walked toward him on soft, bare feet, and knelt on the floor beside the bed. She smiled when her searching gaze landed on his earring, that one glittering diamond that he was wearing again after their visit with Kirby Ellis. No matter how short his hair was, he would never be an ordinary man. She liked that about him, and always had. She had never been able to defy convention the way Del and Noelle did. The years her father had spent pounding her responsibilities into her had not been wasted. Then again, maybe the ability to say to hell with expectations was genetic. Del had it, so did Noelle. Vic was more like the mother she had never known, the woman who had died when Vic was only three. She liked that explanation better than the little voice that sometimes whispered that she was very much like her traditional father.

She placed her folded arms on the bed and watched Del sleep. Heavens, he was gorgeous! His face, his body…her eyes swept down that body and her eyes came to rest on the marking on his chest. It was small, faded, but all too clear. Her smile died slowly. Vic, the name surrounded by the outline of a heart, had been tattooed over Del's own heart. She reached out and touched it, gently tracing the letters in her name. He hadn't forgotten her when he'd walked away. With that name there for him to see every day, he hadn't forgotten her at all.

"I was very young, and very drunk," he said sleepily, his hand reaching up to gently capture her own.

She wanted to cry, for everything that had gone wrong, and in that instant, she hated her father for what he'd done, for what he'd taken from them. In the past she'd tried to reason that even though he was wrong, her father had only done what he'd thought was best. She couldn't fool herself that way any longer. Will Archard was a controlling, manipulative man, and she hated him for what he'd done.

"You can only imagine what it was like showering with a bunch of marines with the name Vic tattooed on my chest," Del teased.

She traced the heart while Del continued to clasp her wrist in his large, warm hand.

"Don't cry, baby," he whispered.

"I'm not," she said as a single tear slipped down her cheek. She sniffled, chased the tears away and looked him in the eye. "Did it hurt?"

"Hell, yes." He managed to give her a lazy grin.

She wondered what he'd say if she told him she wasn't asking about the tattoo.

"Come on," he said, pulling back the sheet and inviting her in. "I'm not ready to get out of bed. Not yet."

Vic gratefully joined Del in the bed, snuggling against him, finding that perfect resting place for her head— there in the crook of his shoulder. And she wondered if when they finally left the bed and this room, the truce they'd called last night would be over.

Vic poured coffee for three and smiled at Shock. "Don't you sleep?" she asked.

"Not much," Shock admitted as he took the mug Vic offered.

"He probably slept half the night, sitting in the car at the end of the road," Del said.

"Did not," Shock muttered defensively. "And if I did take a very short nap, I made sure there was someone wide-awake sitting right beside me."

Del glared.

"Stakeout is the most boring part of the job," Shock argued. "Hey, Vic," he said, eager to change the subject, "that friend of yours, Wanda. Is she…seeing anybody?" The question was accompanied by a waggle of his eyebrows.

"No," Vic answered as she added sugar to her own coffee. "Not at the moment."

"Girl like that—pretty, smart, mouthwatering figure—she probably has to fight men off with a stick." Shock wrinkled his nose.

Del couldn't believe what he was seeing. Shock was nervous. About a woman.

You'd never know it to look at him, but Albert Shockley was never without a woman. He wasn't good-looking by anyone's standards, he wasn't tall or muscular. But he had charm—there was no other word for it—and women came on to him all the time. He had a gift for making each woman feel special.

And he never got nervous. Or serious.

"She has *how* many kids?" Del asked.

Shock shot a narrow-eyed glance Del's way. "Three boys, and I'm sure they're all very well behaved." He turned to Vic. "Right?"

"They…have their moments," she said, apparently trying to soften the blow. "They are *boys,* after all. Seven, nine and ten years old."

"Oh. But…they spend most of the day in school, right?" Shock asked.

Vic wrinkled her nose, trying not to smile. "Summer vacation."

Shock smiled widely. "I'll bet they spend at least part of the summer with their dad. Where does he live?" He looked as if he were hoping for someplace far away from Alabama. Someplace like Alaska.

Vic's smile faded. "Wanda's not divorced. She's a widow."

"Ouch," Shock muttered.

Del's radio saved them all, coming to life with a crackle and a tinny voice. "We have two men headed for the door," a man on the day crew piped in. "No sign that they're armed, one of them is an old guy. What do you want us to do?"

Del pressed the button on the side of the walkie-talkie. "Stand by." He took his pistol from its place at his spine and headed for the front door, and Shock put down his coffee cup and easily slipped his own weapon into his hand. Shock cut into the living room, where he'd be out of sight but ready.

Vic was on Del's heels. "Stay in the kitchen," he ordered.

"I will not!"

He cast her a sharp glance that made her hesitate before continuing to follow him. "It's probably nothing. A salesman or the preacher or a..."

Del looked through the peephole. "Or your father."

Vic went still and white. "He never comes here," she said softly. "Why now?"

He looked down at her. The bastard really had her in knots...it wasn't right. "You want me to get rid of him?"

The change was quick and sure. The color came back to Vic's face, her spine grew rigid and the light in her eyes dimmed. "No." This was Vic prepared to do battle, this was the woman who had learned to get by without anyone's help. He hated that, in a way. He wanted her to lean on him, to ask him to take care of her problems for her. But she was all grown up now and she took care of her own problems. "I'll handle it."

With her chin high she opened the door, poised for battle, steely-eyed and outwardly calm. Inside, he didn't think she was calm at all. She was prepared for the sight of her father, but not for the man who stood behind Will Archard. Her face went white.

"Preston," she said, her facade faltering.

The asshole, live and in person.

Will Archard stepped into the house without being invited, and his eyes immediately lit on Del. "And you are?" he asked, his air superior, his nose out of joint. How could someone who was no more than five foot eight look down at a man who stood a good six inches taller? Archard certainly tried.

"Oh, we've met," Del said, offering his hand. He waited until he had Archard's hand in his before he finished. "But it has been a long time. Del Wilder." He grinned tightly. "Remember me?"

The old man went white himself and his lips thinned.

"Is Noelle here?" Preston asked tightly as he followed Archard into the entryway. "I told her I'd be here this week." He glanced at his watch. "We tee off in twenty minutes. I don't have much time."

"Preston," Archard said, his voice rigid, "this is Del Wilder. I believe you've heard the name."

Preston appeared to be only slightly distressed. But he did offer a meaningful lift of one eyebrow. "I do hope you're not here to stir up trouble." He returned his attention to Vic. "Victoria, is Noelle here?"

"No, she's not," Vic answered. Confused, she glanced from one man to the other. "What do you two want?"

Archard pressed the thumb and forefinger of one hand to the bridge of his nose. "The company picnic is next weekend. Had you forgotten?"

"Yes," Vic said honestly.

"I thought so." Archard's voice told of his despair. "Ryan Parrish will be in town. He'd like to escort you and Noelle—"

"No," Vic interrupted. "Absolutely not."

"It's a family affair, Victoria. You and Noelle *should* be there. How does it look when my only child refuses to be involved in even the smallest way...."

"A picnic," Del said. He'd had enough of this. Not hitting someone was growing more difficult by the second. Unfortunately, that was not an option. "Oh, baby." He draped an arm around Vic's shoulder. "I can't wait. I love a picnic." He laid his eyes on Archard. "Are you providing the beer or should I bring my own?"

"As charming as it would be to include you, Mr. Wilder," Archard said tightly, "this is strictly for employees of Archard Enterprises and their families."

Will Archard liked to intimidate, and probably always had. With his haughty air, his beady eyes...he was accustomed to getting his own way. And he had pushed Vic around for the last time.

"But I am family, Pops," Del said irreverently. "Or have you forgotten."

"You had to tell him, didn't you," Preston said, his comment directed at Vic. "You couldn't just think of what's best for Noelle and leave things as they are. *Were*," he said with a frown. "Please tell me you haven't told Noelle that this miscreant is her father. She'll be mortified.''

Miscreant? Where the hell were these people from?

Del looked down at Vic, who stood close beside him as if she were trying to hide. No wonder she was so afraid. "I could have them arrested," he said.

Vic shook her head softly.

"I'd like to see you try something so ludicrous," Archard seethed.

Del grinned crookedly as he took his ID from his back pocket and flipped the leather case open to display his badge. "Would you really?"

The tension in the air was thick, so heavy he could almost touch it. Archard didn't like to lose; neither did Del.

"Come on, Will, we're going to miss tee off," Preston said. He was, at least, suitable frightened by the sight of Del's badge. "We don't want to make Ryan and Curtis wait."

"No," Del said, taking a threatening step forward. "Don't make your golf buddies wait. That would be *rude.*"

The two backed out of the front door. When the door closed on them, Vic breathed a sigh of pure relief.

Del placed his hands on her shoulders. "It's okay, baby. They're gone."

She shook her head. "Does it strike anyone but me as odd that my father still likes to play golf with the man who…who…"

"They do deserve each other," he said.

Vic was shaken by the brief visit, and he couldn't resist the urge to lean down and kiss her lightly on the forehead, to lay his hand on her shoulder. She didn't want anyone to take care of her; she needed someone to take care of her more than anyone he'd ever met.

Shock appeared, silently coming up behind Vic. He'd been so still and quiet, there in the living room, Del had almost forgotten his partner was in the house.

"Man, what a couple of dweebs. And stiffs! If you shoved lumps of coal up their butts, you'd have diamonds in less than a week."

Vic laughed. Not loud, and not hearty...but she did laugh.

Shock's expression softened as Vic turned away. He wasn't blind to what was going on, what Vic had been through. "Wanda," he said, changing the subject. "She does at least have a mother in town who can baby-sit a lot, right? Right?"

Her father and her ex stopping by had ruined the morning, but Vic refused to allow them to spoil the entire day. Noelle was safe and Del was her lover again. It wouldn't last, she knew that, but while it did she wanted to enjoy the feel and smell and taste of him.

So she dismissed the unpleasantness her visitors had brought with them and left in her heart, and concentrated on more agreeable matters. It was easy to do, when Del kept coming up behind her and touching her, laying his hands on her in a familiar way, kissing her for no reason at all.

She was in the pantry looking for the peanut butter when he came up behind her and pulled the door shut, leaving them in very close quarters with no light but for the dim bulb that shone overhead. He wrapped his arms around her waist and pulled her close, and said the words she didn't want to hear.

"We need to talk."

"No," she said, rising up on her toes to kiss him lightly. "Talking is highly overrated." She and Del did much better when they didn't talk, when they let their bodies communicate without words.

Del absently unbuttoned the top two buttons of her blouse and let his fingers trail lazily between her breasts. "Once Holly shows up, things will start happening fast. Too fast." One finger trailed up to her neck and back down again. "I want this settled before then."

Her heart climbed into her throat. "You want what settled?"

Del laid his eyes on her face. She wished he would smile, but he didn't. She wished he would forget about getting anything *settled* and just kiss her.

He didn't. "You said it was too dangerous for Noelle or anyone else to know that I'm her father. Do you still believe that to be true?"

Vic licked her lips. "Del…"

"Do you?"

She loved her daughter. She would do anything and everything to protect Noelle. But love balanced out a lot of bad stuff. Noelle deserved a father who loved her, a father who would be there when she needed him. If Del could do that… "I think maybe I was wrong," she said, her voice not rising above a whisper. "I think…Noelle would be very lucky to have you as a father. It won't be easy," she added quickly. "Nothing with Noelle is ever easy. She fights everything." Good and bad, right and wrong. "But the two of you are so much alike." More than they knew. Did anyone see it but her? "I have a feeling the two of you are going to butt heads, and when that happens I don't want to be anywhere close by. But the day will come when you'll be close, I just know it.'' She took a deep breath. ''When this is over, we should tell her. Together.''

Del smiled and reached up to hook a strand of hair behind her ear. The move was simple and intimate and unexpectedly arousing. ''And what about you, Vic?'' he asked.

''What about me?'' she whispered. Her heart hammered against her chest, she couldn't breathe. A part of her wanted to kiss Del to silence him, touch him in a way he couldn't resist, and then make love to him right here. Against the wall, on the floor. Anywhere. The physical aspect of their relationship she could handle. It might not last…but she understood it. Anything more than that scared the hell out of her.

But she did nothing but grab a fistful of Del's T-shirt and hold on tight, while she rested her nose against his heart. There, where he had her name carved on his skin, burned into his flesh.

Del wasn't going to let her get off easy. He cupped her chin and made her look him in the eye. ''You need me.''

''I…'' She started to argue, but didn't get far. The normally easy argument died on her lips, and she had to force it, harsh and unyielding. ''I don't need anyone.''

Del didn't seem at all surprised. ''You need me.''

Vic's heart hammered too hard. She didn't need anyone, not anymore. She was all grown up, and if she leaned on Del and he left again…it would kill her. ''I'm not a kid anymore,'' she insisted.

''Neither am I,'' Del countered. ''But that doesn't mean that I don't need you.''

He was talking about physical need, she knew, and that she could handle. ''Now?'' she whispered. ''Here?''

Del smiled and shook his head. ''Well, yes, but…

dammit, Vic, why do you have to make everything so difficult?''

"*Me?*"

"Yes." He leaned down and placed his face close to hers. They stood there eye to eye, nose to nose. A simple shift of her head and they'd be mouth to mouth. "Last night, you said you loved me."

Her heart hitched in her chest. "I did not!" she insisted.

"You did," Del said, not at all offended by her response. "Half-asleep, well loved…" His smile faded. "Did you mean it? Or was it just a…a part of an old dream?"

It would be safest to tell him she hadn't meant it, that she wanted nothing beyond what they'd shared last night. But the words caught in her throat. Did she still love him? As much as she had before, more even. Did they have a chance at something beyond the occasional truce?

Yes, they did. They definitely had *something*. That was the reason she hadn't given any thought to protection since that first night they'd almost made love. Del was maddening at times. He'd turned her world upside down. But he was *not* temporary.

"Del…"

His cell phone rang, and he cursed low and long as he placed Vic on her feet and unclipped the phone from his belt.

"What?"

Vic watched as Del listened to the caller, and his anger was replaced by something else. Surprise, then obvious fear.

"They're not a part of this," he said, his voice low and gravelly. "Whatever you want. Anything…" He looked Vic in the eye, and she didn't like what she saw there. Not at all.

"Let me talk to the kid," he said.

Vic's knees went watery. *Noelle.*

"Two seconds!" he argued when his request was apparently refused. Del's face went white as he listened to the caller.

"Is she okay?" Vic whispered.

Del's answer was a quick nod of his head.

"I want to talk to her." As much as she needed to breathe, she needed to talk to her daughter.

Del shook his head in an abrupt refusal and lifted a finger to silence Vic.

A second later, he hit the button to end the call. "That was Holly. She has Noelle and my mother," he said, forcing calmness into his voice.

"Are they okay?" Vic asked.

Del nodded. "It's me Holly wants." He turned, opened the pantry door and stalked away.

He was going to trade himself for Noelle and Louise, she knew it. "There has to be another way."

He shook his head.

It wasn't fair. She wanted Noelle safe, but she also wanted Del alive and safe and with her. Dammit, why couldn't she ever have both? Her daughter and the man she loved. Two halves of her heart, never whole, always wanting... "I'm going with you."

Del turned on her, furious and determined. "You are not."

"Well, I'm not going to let you go alone," she said sternly. "You're not going without me."

Del turned away and headed for the stairs, took them two at a time and threw open the door to Noelle's room, where Shock slept.

"Holly has Noelle and my mother."

It was all the explanation he needed. Shock was up and dressed and out of the room in a matter of minutes.

Del checked the clip in his pistol, stuffed an extra clip in his pocket and turned to his partner, who was doing the same.

"I want you here," Del said.

"What?"

"Vic's going to try to follow me. I don't care if you have to duct-tape her to a kitchen chair, she doesn't leave this house. Got it?"

"Got it," Shock said.

"No," Vic argued, brushing past Shock to get to Del. Dammit, she couldn't fight them both! Physically, she didn't have a chance. "You need me, and I can't just...I *won't* just sit here and wait."

Del took her by the shoulders and looked her in the eye. "You asked me once to make a promise. You said if I had to choose between protecting Noelle and protecting you, that I'd protect her."

"I remember."

"Don't make me choose," he whispered. "It would be an absolute nightmare to find myself in a position where I had to make that kind of decision. In order to do what needs to be done, I have to know that you're here and safe. Please, Vic. Do this for me."

As much as she wanted to be with him, as much as she needed to go to Noelle...she couldn't argue with his reasoning. If he had to know she was out of harm's way in order to do his job, she'd cooperate.

"All right."

He sighed, long and low. She saw the hint of relief on his tense face, and in that moment she knew she had made the right decision. It would be hell on earth, but she'd stay here and wait.

"I want a gun," she added.

"No," Del said.

"You have more than one," she argued.

"You don't need a gun!"

"But…"

"Until I can be absolutely sure you won't shoot yourself in the foot, I'm not giving you a weapon."

"No one really shoots themselves in the foot!"

Shock cleared his throat and looked really embarrassed, as he casually glanced down at his own right foot.

"We don't have time for this, Vic," Del said.

"I know. Forget it. I'll be fine here." She wondered if she should answer his earlier question now. *Yes, I love you. I never stopped. I love you more today than I did sixteen years ago, and that's saying a lot.*

She said nothing. Del didn't need anything else on his mind, and she didn't want to send him off like that, with a desperate *I love you* that might sound like she was confessing her love because she thought he was never coming back. "Take Shock with you," she said softly. "You're going to need him more than I will."

He shook his head. "No. I have to go alone. Those were the instructions and—" she saw the fear in his eyes, a fear he would never admit to "—I'm following the instructions this time. If I don't…" He couldn't finish that thought. "It's not a chance I'm willing to take, Vic."

She nodded silently, her heart in her throat.

Del was riding off to war again, and this time he was going without the cavalry.

Chapter 12

Tense behind the steering wheel of his Jag, Del sped down the interstate. He'd been wrong, horribly wrong, when he'd said Holly would come after him and Vic, not Noelle. He didn't want to think about the possible consequences of that mistake. How had Holly found the Mississippi farm? He'd been so goddamn careful! Very few people knew where the place was, the security system was first-rate and his mother knew better than to open the door to criminals masquerading as delivery men.

But did Noelle?

Noelle. His daughter. His and Vic's child. He hardly knew her, and still…he'd protect her with his life, if need be. He'd do anything to keep her safe. Just as Vic had, all these years.

Vic was right, she'd been right all along. He couldn't guarantee that no one would ever again go after his family to get to him, and that's what Noelle and Vic were.

His family. *His* woman and *his* child. Was it fair to ask them to put their lives on the line just because they were his? No, it wasn't. They deserved better; they deserved to be safe, always. Yeah, Vic had been right all along.

He couldn't tell Noelle that he was her father. He couldn't tell anyone. The truth of Noelle's parentage would have to remain a dark family secret, a reason for Archard and Preston to look down their pointy, aristocratic noses and sneer. No one else could know. No one.

Del repeated that to himself as he sped down the interstate.

Vic waited fifteen minutes. "You're not actually going to let him go there alone," she said, hands on hips as she faced an antsy Shock.

"He didn't give me any choice."

"Do you always do as you're told?" Vic snapped. "Funny, you never struck me as the obedient sort."

"He wants me here, watching you," Shock argued. "Do I like this? Hell, no. Can I disregard the wishes of my partner because I have an uneasy feeling in my gut? No."

She was experiencing that same uneasy feeling, and had been since she'd watched Del walk out the front door. Knowing Shock had it, too, didn't make her feel any better.

"Noelle is his daughter," she said, trying to make Shock understand the importance of this moment.

"I kinda figured as much," he said, his voice low. "They're similar in too many ways. I mean, there's the eyes and the earring thing and kind of a nose thing going on, but it's more than that. Noelle's got *cojones*. She didn't get that from you, and from what little I've seen of your ex she didn't get balls from his gene pool. Makes sense.'' He shrugged. ''And besides, I knew about you. A little.''

She swallowed hard. ''Del told you about me?''

''No.'' He tapped his fingers over his heart. Of course. The tattoo.

Vic shook her head. ''Del won't be thinking clearly when he goes in there to…to trade himself for Noelle and Louise. He's not thinking straight, and he's going to rush in there and get himself killed.'' Tears sprung to her eyes. ''And he's going to do it *alone*.''

''He doesn't want you there.''

''I know.'' And he was right. She wouldn't put Del in a position where he might be forced to choose. She wouldn't rush in blindly and get in the way. She had to trust Del enough to handle this on his own. For once in her life… ''But what about you? *You* should be with him.''

Shock shook his head. ''Del wants you safe, and that's my job, this time. He wants me to watch over you until this is done.''

''Wouldn't you rather be there, with him?''

''Yeah.''

''So what if we find another place for me to wait this out?'' To hide and wait and worry…and wish she'd told Del that she loved him before he'd left this house.

''Where? I can't leave you alone, and I don't know any of the other agents on this detail well enough to be sure that they're, you know, any good.''

There was only one place she could go. No one would expect her to go there, no one would think to look for her there. ''Take me to my father's house.''

Del didn't bother to park down the driveway and walk to the cottage. There would be no sneaking up on Holly.

She was waiting for him, waiting and watching. For all he knew the dark driveway was lined with men just waiting for him to pull something.

He was taking no chances.

He left the Glock at his spine, not attempting to hide the weapon. Holly wouldn't expect him to arrive unarmed. Once she had the Glock, maybe she wouldn't think to check his boots. He'd hidden a small revolver in the left boot, his knife was sheathed in the right.

Lights were shining in the house, bright and welcoming. From the outside, everything looked normal. Perfectly, sanely normal. It wasn't. Del hadn't prayed for years, but as he stepped onto the porch, he prayed hard and fast. His daughter and his mother were in there. He wanted them safe from harm, now and forever.

A sheriff's deputy should be driving by soon. How soon? They were on a regular drive-by, but since everything looked fine there was no reason for them to stop. Just as well. If a deputy did stop, he wouldn't get far.

How had Holly gotten past the alarm system? Louise obviously hadn't had time to hit the panic button before Holly took her hostage. If she had, he would have heard from the sheriff's department by now. So much for his security system. He'd put so much faith in that system! In bells and whistles and hardware. He should have been here himself. He should have killed Holly when he'd had the chance... Too many should-haves.

All that mattered was getting Noelle and Louise out. Nothing else. When he'd tried to trade himself for Vic, Holly had not lived up to her part of the bargain and let her hostage go. What made him think she would this time?

What choice did he have?

The door swung open before Del reached it. Holly

stood there, pale, thinner than she'd been just a few days ago. And smiling.

Del instinctively reached behind him and drew his Glock. It popped up, the sight trained on Holly's forehead. "If either one of them is hurt, you're dead."

Her smile faded, but not completely. "Come on, Wilder. Put the gun down. You know I'm not here alone."

Del stepped forward and Holly moved back. His weapon didn't drop, not even a fraction of an inch. "The man who shot Tripp in the back of the head?" he snapped. "That's your partner?"

Holly's lower lip trembled, her eyes filled with tears. "When I get my hands on that son of a bitch, he's dead. Tripp made it all the way out to the car on his own, he could have been fixed up. But no, that bastard said we didn't have time to worry with screwups who got themselves shot."

"Who?" Holly had been wounded, too. How had she gotten away? "Who put you up to this?"

"You'll find out soon enough." Holly ignored the gun and led the way to the parlor, where Louise and Noelle were strapped to chairs on opposite sides of the room. They were both bound tightly, but only Noelle had a piece of duct tape over her mouth. Dammit, didn't she know that smart mouth of hers could get her killed?

They'd both been crying, but neither one appeared to be hurt.

A young man Del had never seen before entered from the back of the house, a pistol hanging familiarly in his hand, his eyes flitting from one captive to the other and then to Del. "I didn't see anyone else out there," he said.

"I came alone," Del said, "just as you said. Let them go. Now."

"But this is so nice," Holly said, her smile flitting back. "One big happy family. Grandma, Daddy, fresh-mouthed little girl."

Del remained calm. "I have no idea what you're talking about."

Holly tsked. "Of course you do. Apparently, *she* didn't know but, hey…life is full of surprises."

Del looked at Noelle. Her eyes had gone wide, her face paled and huge tears sprang up fast.

"Where's Mama?" Holly asked. "I thought you might bring her with you. I kinda thought she might insist, since we have the little Wilder here. What did you do, tie her up to keep her away?"

"Something like that," Del muttered.

Holly favored her right side, and occasionally laid a tender hand there. Was that where she'd been wounded?

"Why are you doing this?"

Holly shook her head. "At first, we were just hired help. This man went to Tripp and told him you were an undercover agent. Damn," she mumbled. "I never saw it. Neither did Tripp. We were paid good money to get rid of you and the woman, and it seemed fitting, since you were setting us up. Hell, I would have done it for free."

Not just him, according to Holly, but Vic, too. Was she a bigger part of this than simple bait? "Who?" Del asked again.

"Do you think he gave us his name, moron? Not likely. He said we could call him Bob. That wasn't his real name, I'm pretty sure."

"This Bob killed Tripp?"

Holly nodded, once.

"Then why are you still doing his dirty work?" Del shouted. "Let these two go, and…"

"No," Holly interrupted. "Bob sent us here, since you and Mama are surrounded by cops, and we're supposed to get rid of you ASAP. Once you're gone, Mama will be easy. But things are not going to go as Bob has planned, Wilder. We're just going to reel him in, nice and easy like."

Del's Glock snapped up and he aimed at her forehead again. "This is between us. I want them out of here, now."

Holly didn't move, but her new pal did. He lifted his weapon and aimed it at Noelle. Del's heart almost stopped, but he didn't lower his weapon.

"Not her," Holly reprimanded. "We need the kid. Aim that gun at Grandma. We can shoot her if we have to."

The guy did as he was told and pointed his weapon at Louise's temple.

"Why do you need the kid?" Del asked, not dropping his weapon but swinging it to the side so it was not aimed at anyone. The man who threatened his mother did the same, easing his own weapon aside in an unspoken truce. "She's not a part of this."

"Oh, but she is," Holly said. "When Bob came with us to the cabin that night, he gave us very specific instructions not to hurt the girl. He wants Mama and Daddy dead, but we weren't to touch the kid. I'm not sure why or how, but your daughter is going to bring Bob to me, and when he comes here I'm going to blow his brains out, just like he did to Tripp."

She turned her back on Del. "And when that's done, I don't care what happens to the rest of you."

Vic hadn't asked her father for a favor of any kind in years. She didn't want to owe him, not even in the smallest way. He had a way of totaling up and calling in debts owed him.

But tonight she had no choice. She'd asked for his help for Del and Noelle, not for herself.

He'd been perfectly obliging in allowing her to stay here. She had explained a small portion of the story to this point, and he'd even allowed the agents Del had guarding her to sit on the street outside his house.

She suspected he would not be offering them coffee.

Of course, with her father, nothing was free. He'd had his cook prepare an elaborate dinner she would not be able to choke down, and he'd invited Ryan Parrish to join them.

Ryan was a nice-enough guy, and he was good-looking, in a blond kind of way. Golden hair, blue-green eyes, quick smile. She'd dated him twice a few months ago. Dinner. A movie. Nothing special. Even if she hadn't known her father liked Ryan and hoped for more, she wouldn't have gone out with him again.

He hadn't given up easily, like the others usually did. He called when he was in town, and on occasion he still asked her out, even though she always refused.

Apparently Daddy thought Ryan would made a great second husband. He was in and out of Huntsville, working for Archard Enterprises as a consultant. A consultant. As far as Vic could tell that meant he played a lot of golf, traveled frequently and worked only when the spirit moved him.

"This is nice," Ryan said, shooting a grin Vic's way.

"We're so glad you could join us," Will Archard said, as if this was *their* home and *they* had invited him. Her stomach was in knots. What was happening right now? Shock had promised to call when there was news, but there was no telling how long that would be.

What would she do if they were hurt? Or killed? Not just Del, not just Noelle…but both of them. She understood why Del didn't want her there, but dammit, that was where she belonged. With her daughter and the man she loved. Fighting, if necessary.

She became vaguely aware that her father was calling her name. Not Vic, like her friends and acquaintances, but Victoria. Only he and Preston called her Victoria. Vic was much too undignified for them. She lifted her head and found her father and Ryan staring at her. "Yes?"

"Is there something wrong with your shrimp?"

She looked at the untouched food on her plate. "No. I'm just not hungry." He didn't know that Noelle had been taken hostage. He hadn't even bothered to ask where his granddaughter was, even though he knew there was trouble. It was unnatural. Cold and unfeeling and…inhuman. Her father was a monster. Her worst fear was that deep inside she was like him.

"Excuse me," the monster said. "I just remembered, I have an important phone call to make. Ryan, keep an eye on Victoria for me. She doesn't seem to be feeling well."

He was so transparent. Her father liked Ryan, he approved of the man as a suitor for his only child. And why not? Ryan was a great golfer and as big a snob as Will Archard himself.

"You don't have to entertain me," Vic said, her voice low and shaky. She didn't want to be here. If she couldn't be with Del, she wanted to be alone. Preferably with her head beneath the covers. She needed to hide, to cocoon herself against the world.

Ryan's smile softened. "You don't look well. Is there anything I can do?"

Vic shook her head.

"I wish you would let me help you."

Again, Vic shook her head.

"How's Noelle?" he asked, his voice bright as he tried to strike up a conversation.

Anything else. She might be able to choke out a polite conversation about *anything else*. Not Noelle. Not when she didn't know what was happening.

Vic pushed her chair back and left the dining room with a muttered apology. She couldn't stand this. She would not sit there and make small talk while the man she loved and their daughter were in danger.

She didn't expect Ryan to follow her, but he did. He caught her as she began to climb the stairs. His hand fell heavily on her shoulder.

"Victoria...Vic," he amended. "Something's obviously wrong. Let me help?"

"You can't," she said without turning to look at him. She shrugged gently, and his hand dropped from her shoulder.

She'd never had any illusions about Ryan. He wasn't persistent because he felt anything special for her; he wanted to be a part of the Archard family, a part of the Archard fortune.

"It's painfully obvious that you don't care for me the way I care for you," he said gently, "but maybe I can be your friend. You look like you could use a friend, Vic."

She turned. Since Ryan stood on the step below her, they were nose to nose, eye to eye. "Fine. If you want to be my friend, you'll keep my father away from me for the rest of the evening. I'm tired, I'm worried and I don't have the heart to do battle with him tonight.''

''I understand,'' he said softly. ''I don't suppose you can tell me why you're so worried?''

She shook her head and turned to climb the stairs, to hide in the room where she'd lived the first eighteen years of her life. It hadn't changed since she'd had it remodeled at the age of fifteen. Dark antique furniture, pale yellow spread and curtains, a few collectible dolls arranged artfully on a shelf on the south wall, her first decent painting—yellow roses in a white vase—framed and hanging on the north wall. In the years since she'd left here, her father had changed nothing. It was just another room in a house much too big for one man. Sentiment certainly didn't keep him from redecorating the room.

When she was in the bedroom with the door closed and locked behind her, she went not to the bed but to the closet. Her things, remembrances from childhood, were stored in boxes stacked high on the top shelf. She reached for the white box, moving two other boxes aside to reach it. After all these years, she still remembered exactly where it was.

She sat cross-legged on the bed and opened the box. On top there were a couple of certificates she'd won for her artwork, but they were here strictly as camouflage. Beneath the certificates were her memories of Del, all neatly stored. There were a couple of notes, sweet notes that had been passed in school. A Polaroid of the two of them, taken at a church dance. God, they looked so young and so ignorantly happy. She set the photo aside and picked up a blue golf ball, long ago taken from a miniature golf course. Their first real date. A pressed flower, another photo—just Del, this time—and at the bottom of the box another sheet of paper, folded in half.

She unfolded the crisp paper and looked down at Del's face. Why did this sketch she'd done herself feel more real to her than the fading photographs? Because it had been done with love, all her love, more love than she'd known she possessed. This was her Del, young and strong, beautiful as only someone caught between youth and adulthood can be. When she'd drawn this, they'd both thought they had their whole lives ahead of them, and they'd been so sure they would spend that life together. They'd had less than one month, twenty-nine days...and she had never felt so alive since then.

If they got through this, she was going to start over. She would be brave this time, risk anything and everything to have what she wanted most of all. The woman she had become always played it safe. She didn't risk her heart, her life...she took no risks at all. The woman she wished she had become could be fearless. She could tell Del she loved him and bring the two people she loved most together. Del and Noelle. They were hers. They were each other's, too.

"I love you," she whispered to the sketch in her hands. "Bring our daughter home." She touched the smudged pencil marks that formed his long, straight hair. "Come home safe."

He still wasn't sure exactly what Holly wanted, besides seeing *Bob* dead. Maybe she didn't know what she wanted, either. She was feverish, frantic, and the way she waved that gun around...anything was possible.

Del lowered his weapon. He didn't want bullets flying in here, not with Noelle and Louise bound and helpless on either end of the room. "I tell you what. You let them go, and I'll help you find and dispose of Bob."

Holly laughed. "I'm not teaming up with a cop."

Del shrugged. "He killed Tripp, he tried to kill me and Vic, sounds to me like we have a common enemy here. That's all that matters. What difference does it make what I do when I go to work?"

"You want to arrest him," Holly said with a sneer.

"I want him dead."

He didn't like the way she swayed on her feet. "Sit down," he ordered.

Holly did not take kindly to being pushed around. "Kiss my…"

"Sit down before you keel over," Del snapped. "I don't know who Bob is, I don't even have a clue. You've seen him. You can help me find him. I don't need you passing out on me now." He didn't need her dying on him, either. She was the only link to this Bob, the man who wanted him and Vic dead, the man who wanted Noelle alive. A chill crawled up his spine. "Just sit." He holstered his gun, and the guy Holly had hired to help her lowered his until it was pointed at the floor. Finally.

"We'll get you to a doctor," Del said. "Someone who can be discreet. Once you're on the mend, you'll help me find this bastard."

Holly didn't sit, but there was a hint of concession on her pale face. "Why should I believe you?"

"He keeps trying to kill me. What more do you need?" He didn't add that the knowledge that this Bob wanted Noelle alive gave him the willies, or that he would do anything to protect his family.

"Boyce," Holly nodded to the young man as she finally took Del's advice and sat on the sofa. "Take a walk around the house and make sure there are no other cops lurking around out there.''

Boyce obeyed with a curt nod, leaving the parlor, walking through the kitchen, then exiting out the back door.

''I came alone,'' Del said as the echo of the back door closing reached them.

''I know.'' Holly laid her head back. ''But I don't trust Boyce, not a hundred percent.'' She laid watery eyes on him. ''I want Bob dead.''

''So do I.''

''Why does he want you and this Victoria dead, and your daughter alive?''

His heart hitched, and he glanced at a frightened Noelle. ''I don't know.''

''Is she, like, rich or something?''

Del's heart dropped to his knees, and a possibility he had never even considered came together. He had never suspected… He couldn't voice his suppositions here, in front of Noelle. What if he was wrong?

But if Vic was dead and there was no way Del could come back and claim his daughter, Noelle would be sole heir to Will Archard's fortune. And wouldn't it be convenient for the asshole to step back into her life and take over?

Holly had called Vic *Victoria*. Very few people called her by her full name. Her father. Her ex.

The back door opened and closed, and footsteps clipped across the kitchen floor.

''All clear?'' Holly asked, raising her voice just slightly.

Silence.

''Boyce!'' Holly rose carefully to her feet.

The footsteps came closer. Boyce was wearing tennis

shoes, but the footsteps that sounded in the hallway were hard, as the soles of a boot or a heavy shoe clipped across the floor.

Del gripped the handle of his Glock and raised it smoothly. His mouth went dry; the hairs on the back of his neck stood up.

Holly lifted her own gun and aimed at Noelle.

"No," Del muttered.

"He's not getting her," Holly said. "She's what he wants, and I'm going to take her away from him the way he took Tripp from me."

"Don't make me shoot you," Del said softly as he took aim. His heart climbed into his throat. If he shot Holly now and she instinctively pulled the trigger, Noelle would be hit. And even if her aim wavered, he didn't have a clean shot that didn't put Noelle in the line of fire.

"I'm already dead," Holly mumbled.

She raised her weapon another inch, just as Shock appeared in the doorway, his own weapon drawn. "Drop it!"

It was not the voice Holly expected to hear. She spun around, and when she did, Del fired.

Chapter 13

Del drew his knife, dropped down beside Noelle and began to cut away the duct tape. Shock had placed a quick call on his cell phone and was kneeling beside Holly, assessing the damage.

"Is she dead?" Del asked softly.

"Not yet," Shock said as the front door opened and half a dozen deputies stormed in. Sheriff Warren Timberlake went immediately to Louise and began to cut her loose, a string of softly spoken profanity accompanying each slice of his knife.

Noelle murmured behind the duct tape covering her mouth, and Del stopped cutting to carefully remove it. There were tears and fire in her eyes. "You...you goon. This is all your fault."

"I know," he said softly.

Her lower lip trembled, but she stilled the telling sign quickly. "I hope you're happy. You've ruined my life."

The accusation cut to the core, even though he real-

ized that Noelle was only lashing out at the closest, easiest target for her anger. "We'll talk about that later,"
he said.

Noelle looked as if she were searching for something
suitably caustic to say. Her nose twitched, the fire in her
eyes flared to life again. But before she could lash out
again, the fire eased. "You cut your hair," she said,
instead of calling him a thug or a goon and suggesting
something anatomically impossible.

"Yeah."

"Why?"

"Because you said I looked like a reject from the
seventies," he admitted, grumbling as he cut the last of
the bonds at her legs.

"That's *not* why," she said, her voice low and angry.
"I'm quite certain you don't give a damn about what I
think."

"Maybe I do." He still had so much to say. Noelle
had found out he was her father in the worst possible
way...how could that be fixed? Could it ever? Now was
not the time or place. "Stay right here," he said as he
cut the last of the duct tape away and glanced at his
mother. She was busy explaining to a very concerned
sheriff how Noelle had turned off the security system so
she could go out and see the horses, and how the kid
had turned off the telephone number blocking system to
call a boyfriend who had caller ID that rejected call
blocking.

So that's how they'd found Noelle. A phone call, a
number traced...and they were here.

When the sheriff cast a cutting glance to Noelle and
began to speak sharply, Louise reached out, took the
lawman's chin in her hand, and said, "Stop that, Warren.
If you have something to say, you can say it to me."

Warren? His mother had some explaining to do. Again.

Del turned to Shock. "What the hell are you doing here?" he snapped as the paramedics moved in and began to stabilize Holly. "You're supposed to be watching Vic!"

"I know," he grumbled. "She came up with another plan and sent me after you."

Del cursed, low, but not low enough.

"Delaney Wilder," his mother said sharply. "Watch your language."

He glanced at her just long enough to decide that she and the sheriff looked much too chummy.

Del turned back to Shock. "What kind of plan? The kind of plan where you do exactly what I told you not to do?"

"She's at her dad's house. Detail out front. Security system on." Del glanced at Noelle, who no doubt now knew of her mistakes. Mistakes that could have gotten her killed. They needed to have a nice long talk about that. At the moment, a shaking Noelle was telling a paramedic to get lost—in her own charming way.

Her dad's house. Preston Lowell and Will Archard were golf buddies. Preston still worked for his father-in-law. He could walk right in, and no one would think twice.

"Give me your phone," Del snapped, offering his palm to Shock, who handed the cell phone over without question. "Noelle, what's your grandfather's phone number?"

"I don't know, and if I did I wouldn't tell you."

"You don't know your grandfather's phone number?" He was certain for a moment that she was just being difficult.

"I don't call him, you moron! Ever! He hates me, and at least now I know why!" Her shouting silenced the room for a few uncomfortable minutes.

Shock quietly rattled off a phone number, and then added, "I told Vic I'd call, but I'm pretty sure she'd rather hear from you."

Del dialed the number, and as it rang he laid his eyes on Noelle. He had no idea what to do next. He had finally decided that it wasn't safe or right to tell her he was her father, and then she finds out this way, trussed to a chair with a gun to her head, the news delivered as if it were a big joke.

Deep inside he was glad she knew. He only wished she'd heard the news from him and Vic.

"Hello." Archard's voice was tight, as usual.

"Put Vic on the phone."

Archard's response was cool and sharp.

"I doubt very much that she's resting," Del said, his own voice as calm as he could manage. "If you don't put her on the phone now, I'm going to come to your house and kick your scrawny butt all the way to Nashville. Any questions?"

A moment later, Vic was on the line, her voice breathlessly short.

"We're all fine," he said, getting the news Vic wanted and needed out of the way quickly. "I'm bringing Noelle back tonight." God knows sleep would be impossible, and besides, the long driveway would give him and his daughter time to talk things out. "Stay where you are, but Vic..." He turned away so Noelle couldn't see, stepped away so maybe she wouldn't hear. "Steer clear of Preston," he said lowly.

"What?"

"Your ex," he said. "I have a bad feeling about him."

"Join the club. Is Noelle there? Can I talk to her?"

"In a minute. I'm serious, Vic. I think Preston is behind this whole thing."

"That doesn't make sense."

"I'll explain later."

Someone tapped him on the shoulder, and he turned to look down into Noelle's defiant eyes. Without saying a word, she asked for the phone. Palm out, eyes condemning.

"Mom?" she said, a touch of the child in her voice as she spoke to her mother.

She listened for a few seconds, and then she asked sharply, "Why didn't you tell me about Wilder?" He could tell by looking at her face that she fought back tears.

"I don't want to talk about this later, I want to talk about it *now!*" A couple of tears slipped down her cheeks. "Yes, I'm really fine," she said quietly. "Considering that I spent the afternoon and most of the evening duct-taped to a chair, and some crazy woman pointed a gun at my head more than once, and I found out that some psycho narc who ran out on you years ago is my real father and…" She stopped suddenly, no doubt interrupted by Vic. And then she handed the phone to Del. "I'm finished," she said harshly.

Del told Vic they'd be there in a few hours and ended the call.

Noelle glared at him. "I am not getting in any car with you. I'll stay here with…with…" She struggled a moment. Had she just realized that Louise was her grandmother? "Maybe your freak of a partner can drive me back to Huntsville, but I'm not going home, and I'm not going to Grandpa's house. He can drop me off at Chris's house."

"Who's Chris? A girlfriend?"

Her eyes hardened. "My boyfriend, moron."

Boyfriend. He was definitely not ready for this.

Noelle kept her eyes on the dark road and her arms crossed over her chest. She wasn't going to look at *him.* Not now, not ever.

All her life, she'd felt like a freak. She wasn't like her mother, she wasn't like her...the man she'd thought was her father. She was different, and she'd always known it. She hated being different sometimes.

Now she knew why. She was just like *him.*

"Noelle, we need to talk," Wilder said.

"Go ahead," she said, trying to sound disinterested. "Talk all you want. I have nothing to say."

He took a deep breath. They hadn't even made it to the interstate yet. She'd be trapped in this car for hours!

"I didn't want you to find out that way."

"Apparently, you didn't want me to find out at all," she said. "That's cool. I don't like you, either."

"No, I wanted to tell you, but...I just found out about you a few days ago. I didn't know..."

"So, you're going to blame this all on Mom. Fine. Right now I don't like her any more than I like you."

"I'm not trying to blame anyone. What happened was just...it was no one's fault."

"So you're going to tell me that the best explanation you can come up with is *tough luck, kiddo. That's the way the cookie crumbles?*"

He sighed, long and exasperated. Good. She wanted him to be exasperated, she wanted him to suffer.

"We can't go back and undo anything, but I'd like to

make up for lost time now. I want to get to know you, do stuff together, maybe…''

"Please," Noelle interrupted. "Save your breath."

"I never knew I had a little girl," he said softly.

"You're not going to come in here and play daddy all of a sudden," she said sharply, "and I'm not going to be your *little girl.* I don't expect anything from you, I don't *want* anything from you." She already knew what it was like to be pushed aside. She wasn't really anxious for it to happen again. "Let's face it, Wilder. You're going to hang around until you get tired of having wild monkey sex with my mother, and then you're going to split again."

"Noelle!"

"Well, it's the truth."

"It is not." That sigh, again. "I want to get to know you. I want you to be a part of my life."

Sounded nice, but she knew better. Besides, she didn't even like Wilder, right? He was a narc, and he was probably just as unpleasantly surprised to find out about her as she had been to find out he was her father. No, if he was being nice to her it was because he felt obligated… or because he thought playing Daddy with her would make his Vic happy.

"Well, get over it," she muttered. "You're not a part of my life, and you're not going to be. You're…sperm. That's all," she added. "You're a long-lost sperm donor."

He was speeding, and he knew it. Didn't care. Sperm donor? Wild monkey sex? Boyfriend?

"This Chris," Del said, trying to sound nonchalant. "What's he like?"

Out of the corner of his eye, he saw Noelle look at him. "What do you care?"

"Just curious."

"He's cute," she said with a shrug. "And funny. He makes me laugh."

Del wanted to kill him already. Cute *and* funny. "How long have you two...I mean, how long has Chris been your boyfriend?"

"Three months."

Too long. *Way* too long. "What do you two do when you go out?" He tried to sound so damned cool.

"We have orgies at his house," Noelle said sharply. "Followed by drinking and drugs and then more orgies."

Del swerved to the side of the road and brought the Jag to an abrupt stop. He turned to face his daughter, to see her too-hard face illuminated by the dashboard lights.

"Just kidding," she said, her face softening. "Jeez, can't you take a joke? What do you care what I do for fun, anyway?"

"Answer my question," he said in the voice no one dared to ignore.

"I don't have to tell you anything," she insisted. "My life is none of your business. If I want to—"

"Your life is my business," he seethed. "I don't care if you like it or not." He tried to calm himself down. "I know you had a bad day."

"That's the understatement of the year," she muttered.

"And if giving me a hard time helps you deal with that, then I can live with it. Maybe." He wanted to reach across and touch her shoulder, maybe her cheek, but he didn't dare. "Just don't tell me your life is none of my business." He took a deep breath. "Chris?"

"We go to the movies with friends," she said, cocking her head to one side. "Sometimes we go out for pizza. We rent movies and watch them with his little brother. Happy?"

"A little happier than I was a few minutes ago," he confessed. Now was not the time to back down, and he wanted—no, he *needed* to know. "Noelle, are you...I mean, I know you were yanking my chain about the orgies, but...I know kids these days think they can do anything they want, that they're all grown up." He almost choked. Had he really just used the phrase *kids these days?* He took a deep breath and continued. "You're only fifteen, Noelle, and these days it's downright dangerous..." His heart jumped. This was no fun at all. "Fifteen is very young, even though it might not seem that way to you...."

Noelle held up a hand and presented her palm to him. "Okay, are you actually trying to ask me if I'm a virgin?"

His stomach dropped. "Yes."

"Like it's any of your business."

"Noelle..."

"I've known you're my...my sperm donor for a couple of hours, and you think you can come in here and ask me personal questions that are *none of your business* and then expect me to answer them?"

"You don't have to call me daddy, you don't have to like me." Though the knowledge that she didn't made his heart hurt a little. "But dammit, I expect you to take care of yourself. You're too good to fall for a line from some charming fifteen-year-old Romeo...."

"Chris is seventeen," she interrupted.

"He's dead," Del muttered.

"Can we just go?" Noelle said with a wave of her hand. "I don't want to be stuck in this car with you any longer than I have to."

Del took a deep breath and pulled back onto the road. This parent business was going to be harder than he'd expected.

He'd considered bringing his mother with them, but she and the sheriff had insisted that she stay behind. Del figured he'd left her in good hands. Holly had been whisked off to the hospital and Shock was rounding up a picture of Preston Lowell for Holly to identify, when she came to. No telling how long that would be, and if she died…he didn't want to think about that.

Right now he wanted to shelter Vic and Noelle, hold them close, protect them…and dammit, from everything he'd seen, neither of them wanted his protection.

He'd never been so confused, not when it came to knowing what was right. His world was black-and-white, good and bad. He wanted to do what was right, where Vic and Noelle were concerned, but he didn't know how.

They had been driving for fifteen long, silent, uncomfortable minutes when Noelle spoke again.

"Yes, you geek," she said softly. "My mother's lectures have not been totally wasted. I'm still a virgin. I figure I should wait until I'm sixteen."

Del gripped the wheel. Was Noelle serious, or was she trying to get a rise out of him again? Neither, he decided. She was trying to give him a heart attack. She'd almost succeeded. "We'll talk about it on your birthday," he growled. "No, we'll talk about it a day or two before your birthday."

"Like you'll be here that long," she scoffed.

He took his eyes off the road long enough to glare at her. "I'll be here."

It was getting close to midnight, and they were finally nearing Huntsville. Noelle had wanted to sleep on the trip up the interstate, but she hadn't been able to. Her mind was spinning, and she could still remember what it had been like when that crazy woman came through the back door and grabbed her. She'd been so scared...and she hadn't liked it.

Wilder drove silently, no more anxious to resume their conversation than she was. Geek. Narc. Thug. She glanced his way. He didn't look so much like a thug with his hair short. Had he really cut it because she said he looked like a reject? No way. He couldn't possibly care what she thought.

But he had asked if she was a virgin, and he'd been really pissed when she let him think she wasn't. Not that Chris hadn't tried, but she was no dummy. If he loved her like he said he did, he'd wait. If he didn't love her, better to find out now than later.

Her dad...Preston Lowell, who was *not* her dad...had never asked about Chris, or what she did when she went out or if she was a virgin. Not because the subject was too uncomfortable for him, but because he didn't care. He didn't care and he never had, and now she knew why. In a way she was relieved. She'd seen the way other fathers treated their daughters, and it was more like the way Wilder treated her in the past couple of hours than her...than Preston ever had.

"Do you love my mother?" she blurted out. Obviously she took him by surprise. The car swerved, just a little.

"What?"

Noelle scoffed. That was answer enough. "I'll take that as a no." Which meant that no matter what he said, Wilder wouldn't be here when her birthday rolled around. He probably wouldn't be here a month from now.

He drove silently for a couple of minutes, the Jag steady once again. "I don't know," he said. "I want to be honest with you, I don't want to…toss words around like they don't mean anything."

"Save the explanations, Wilder. It was a very simple yes-or-no question."

"Not so simple," he muttered.

"Forget it."

He didn't. "Sixteen years ago, I loved your mother so much it hurt," he said softly. "She was in my head all the time. Every time I saw her, I was amazed by the…the power she had over me."

Noelle snorted. "That's lust, narc. Even I know that."

"No," he said sharply. "It was much more than that."

"Then why didn't it last?"

"I think it did."

She was more confused than ever. "So do you love her or not?"

He took another of those long, deep breaths. "I think I should save this part of the conversation for her."

"Coward," she breathed.

"Noelle," he said, turning onto the road that would take them to her grandpa's house. "I love you."

Her heart jumped in her chest, and there were butterflies she refused to acknowledge in her stomach. "Yeah, right," she muttered.

"It's true."

Noelle turned her face away to look at the houses they

passed, so Wilder wouldn't see the tears in her eyes. *Now* who was the geek?

Hell, she liked Wilder. She wasn't ready to admit to anything more than that, but there was something about him. Something she identified with. She wasn't a geek, like he was, but still...sometimes she felt like he understood her in a way no one else ever would. That he really did, deep down, care about her...for now. Preston Lowell had never told her he loved her, not once, not even when she tried so hard to make him feel something. Anything.

She was terrified that if she let herself love Wilder, he'd leave. That if she came to depend on him, one morning she'd get up and he'd be gone. For good. There was no way she could tell him that maybe, just maybe, she could love him, too. Still, she didn't want to let the moment pass without saying *something*.

"The way you told Grandpa you'd kick his ass if he didn't put Mom on the phone," she said as Wilder pulled the Jag to a halt at the curb, behind another car where two men sat. "That was cool."

Tears sufficiently dried, she looked at Wilder. He smiled widely. "Thanks, kiddo."

Her own smile faded. "Just because you're my father, that doesn't mean you can call me kiddo. I'm too old for that."

"Okay, I like *ladybug* better, anyway."

"That's even worse!"

He didn't look at all disturbed by her outburst. "First time I saw you, it was in that picture where you're dressed as a ladybug. I kinda liked it, that's all."

"I would be absolutely mortified if you called me kiddo or ladybug...in front of anyone else. And I do mean anyone! Same goes for sweetie, sugar and every other cute little nickname you can think of.'' When they were alone, though, maybe she wouldn't mind so much.

Wilder reached out and took her face in his big, gentle hands, leaned forward and kissed her on the forehead. ''Sorry,'' he said softly. ''I'll try to remember, I promise. This is just all so new to me.''

It's new to me, too, Noelle thought as Wilder backed away.

Vic opened the door before Del and Noelle reached it, and rushed out onto the porch to greet her daughter with a big hug. She held on too tight and expected Noelle to protest at any moment. She didn't. Noelle's own arms snaked around and held on, in an uncharacteristic display of emotion.

And then Del was there, arms around them both as he guided them inside and closed the door.

''I was so worried,'' Vic admitted as she backed away from Noelle and stroked her cheek with one hand.

''It's okay,'' Noelle said softly. ''Wilder is pretty handy to have around, I guess. I'm glad he showed up when he did.''

Del looked as surprised as Vic felt. Noelle had been so angry when they'd spoken on the phone, and rightfully so, that she'd expected this homecoming to be difficult. Noelle was subdued. Was she just tired? Or had the day's events drained her?

''Let's go,'' Del said sharply.

''Not so fast.''

Then all three turned to watch Will Archard walk into the foyer, still dressed in his suit as if he expected to be called to work after midnight, his white hair perfectly styled, his face a picture of miserliness. The man might have a fortune in the bank, but he couldn't afford a smile, a kind gesture.

"I don't know what you've dragged my daughter and granddaughter into, but I think they should stay here, for the time being."

Del's jaw tightened. With a full-blown five o'clock shadow and eyes as hard as a deep blue stone, he looked not at all agreeable. "No," he said simply.

"I believe they'll be safer here than they could ever be with you," Archard said, the words a blatant insult.

"Do you really?" Del asked, as if he knew… something. He had warned her about Preston, told her he thought her ex might be behind everything that had happened. She couldn't imagine how, but if Del believed it to be true, it probably was.

They could have a battle, right here in the foyer, and neither man would give an inch. Vic stepped between them. "I appreciate the offer, Dad, but Noelle and I are going home."

"It's a mistake," he said. "He's never been good enough for you. And now he's going to drag you into his squalid life and put you and Noelle in danger."

"Maybe that's a risk I'm willing to take," Vic said softly. She turned, just as her father reached out—not for her, but for Noelle. He grabbed Noelle's arm and held on tight.

"Good Lord," he said, as he finally noticed the change in his granddaughter. "Your hair! How could you do such a stupid thing!"

Del stepped forward. "Let go of my daughter," he said, his voice low and commanding.

Archard did as he was told.

"And if you ever call her stupid again," Del added

as Noelle stepped away from her grandfather and to Del's side, "I'll..."

The threat hung in the air, unfinished but more than clear enough.

"You'll kick his ass, right?" Noelle whispered as she took a single, telling step closer to Del, so obviously searching for the protection no other man had ever offered her.

Del smiled. "Something like that." He draped one arm around Noelle and the other around Vic. "Let's go home."

Chapter 14

Del stood in the doorway and watched a sleeping Noelle. He'd never been so scared in his life as he had been when he'd watched Holly aim a gun at her head. How did you protect a child from the Hollys of the world? The Archards? The Chrises?

He'd added to the guard on the house. There were now six men posted instead of four, and it would remain that way until Preston Lowell was arrested. If he could've arranged it, he'd have put an army out there.

When Vic came up behind him and placed a gentle arm around his waist, he wasn't surprised. Without taking his eyes from Noelle, he draped an arm over Vic's shoulder.

"She's going to be fine," Vic whispered.

Again, Vic was protecting him. Comforting him. Being there for him in a way no one else ever had. "I know. Any other kid would have fallen apart, after going through what Noelle's been through today, but not her. She's strong.''

"Like you," Vic whispered.

He glanced down at her. She had her own strength, she just refused to see it.

Noelle seemed to think that he would hang around until he got tired of sleeping with Vic, and then he'd move on. At the moment, he couldn't imagine moving on, ever. Did he love her? Maybe. Then again, maybe this was just lust, adrenaline and memory.

Hell, he didn't know what love was anymore. At eighteen it had been easy. Eighteen-year-olds didn't know anything beyond the moment, and the moment had been fine. Very fine. At thirty-four everything was more complicated.

"Come on," Vic whispered, reaching out to take the doorknob in her hand and very gently close Noelle's door. "You need to get to sleep yourself."

He didn't know if he could sleep. Until Preston was arrested, until he knew his daughter and Vic were safe…how was he supposed to sleep, ever again?

He half expected Vic to hand him a pillow and blanket and direct him to the couch. After all, Noelle was here and Vic had always been very conscious of appearances. But instead of sending him downstairs, Vic took his hand and led him to her bedroom, where she closed the door and locked it.

When Vic turned around, he was there. Waiting. He took her face in his hands, tilted her face up to his and kissed her, soft and sweet, then soft and not-so-sweet. He rocked his thumb against her cheeks, then moved his hands down to her neck, where his thumb rocked again, against her pulse, this time.

While they kissed, Vic unbuttoned his shirt and laid

her hand against his chest, over his heart, over the tattoo that bore her name. Her palm rested there for a moment, while their tongues danced, and then skimmed down his ribs to rest at his side.

He held her close, lifted her off her feet and swung her around so he could carry her to the bed. She wrapped her legs around him, holding on, teasing him with her body pressed so close to his erection. He should be exhausted, and he was. He was. But right now, all he could think about was getting inside Vic. Then he would sleep. Maybe.

Did he love her? He loved the way she felt in his arms, the way she smiled at him sometimes, the way she protected their daughter. At moments like this, it would be easy to say he loved her. He wanted her, he needed her, and if that seemed like love…maybe it was.

Vic helped Del undress her, shedding everything there by the bed and tossing the clothes aside, before going through the same process with him. She wanted to see him naked, she wanted to touch every inch of him and make sure no one had hurt him tonight. His shirt came off, and she ran her hands along his ribs, around his waist, up his back. He was hard and warm, tough as nails and still gentle as the velvet night.

She unfastened his jeans, lowered the zipper and slipped her hands beneath the waistband. She couldn't touch him enough. He was real, and warm, and here, and she didn't want to let him go.

When his clothes had joined hers on the floor, he lowered her to the bed, hovering above and all around her, cradling her in his arms.

"I was so afraid you wouldn't come back," she whispered. *Again.*

Del kissed her, his wicked lips lingering over hers. "I'm here."

It was easy to think about being brave, to imagine opening her heart without reserve, without fear. Reality was much harder. After he'd left she'd wished she'd told him how she felt. At the moment, the words stuck in her throat. "I'm glad you're here," she said. That was true enough. It was also the easy way out.

"Me, too." Del didn't rush, but took his time touching and tasting her. His lips lingered on her throat and her breasts, his hands caressed her gently, as if he were afraid she might break. For a few moments she lay there and savored his touch and his heat, and then she laid her hands on Del and once again let those hands explore, looking for wounds she knew he didn't have, her fingers dipping and fluttering, tracing ridges and valleys. They lay on their sides, facing each other, kissing and cuddling, arousing and tasting.

He made her breathless, he made her lose control. In the dark, with his body close to hers, she could forget everything ugly that had happened before, everything ugly that went on outside this room.

Her body throbbed, she wanted Del so badly. She lifted one leg and draped it over his, bringing him a little closer. His fingers stroked gently, intimately, and she almost shattered at the simple touch. Everything else faded until there was only this; the way he aroused her, the way she fit against him. The way they came together. But she didn't guide him to her, she didn't rush to have him inside her. This, the touching and the waiting, was too beautiful to hurry.

Del rolled her onto her back, languid, never taking his mouth from hers. She kept her arms around his neck, holding on as if for dear life. He was hers. He belonged to her and always had. And she belonged to him. It was scary, profound and wonderful, all at the same time.

He took his mouth from hers and rose up, raking his hands down her body, spreading her legs and kneeling between them to watch the way his hands looked on her body in the moonlight. His hands raked up her inner thighs, the movement slow, the touch tender. He gripped her hips, brushed his thumbs across her hipbones and dragged her closer to him. Her legs wrapped around his hips and she pulled him nearer, until his erection brushed her damp center.

"You're so beautiful," he whispered, his hands on her body, his eyes on her face. "More beautiful than I remembered, and my memories of you..." he shook his head and grazed his big hands up her thighs again. "There's no one in the world like you, Vic."

She reached out for Del, needing his mouth against hers as much as she wanted him inside her. Her body arched, her mouth reached.

He entered her slowly, pressing into her an inch at a time. Vic closed her eyes and savored the sensation, reached out to draw him down to her. She wanted him close, everywhere. She wanted his body against her, inside hers, all around. She wanted his mouth to mate with hers the way his length did. She wanted everything, and he gave it to her.

Too soon, she came with a soft cry. Her body leaped, her inner muscles lurched and squeezed, as she found the most intense release she had ever known. And Del came with her, with a soft cry of his own and a growl of her name.

Depleted, they lay there, entwined, unable to move. Vic finally lifted a hand and caressed Del's hair. Brave.

Could she really and truly become the woman she wanted to be?

"I love you," she whispered.

Del lifted his head and looked down at her. She couldn't read his expression, even though she could see his face well enough. "You only say that when I'm inside you. When your heart is still pumping hard and your breath won't come. When I'm wearing your sweat and you're wearing mine. That's not love."

Not the response she'd been hoping for, but real and true bravery wasn't supposed to be easy. "Maybe I should tell you again, later."

"This is nice," Del whispered. "This is good. Do we really want to mess it up with...love?"

"Yes."

He left her then, withdrawing, rolling away, coming to rest on his side and taking her in his arms.

"You love Noelle...." Vic began.

"That's a whole different kind of love," Del argued, his voice low and his hands possessive.

"I know." Vic cuddled against him, buried her head against his chest and took a nice, long breath, filling her lungs with Del. "I just want you to understand that... we're not a package deal. You don't have to romance me to get close to Noelle. You can see her as much as you want. You can be a part of her life, even if you're not a part of mine. I don't want you to think—"

"Vic, baby," he interrupted, "tonight I'd rather not *think* at all." He tightened his arms a little. "Just sleep with me. Hold me. And if I wake in the night..."

"I'll be here," she said softly. "I'll be right here."

Del slipped from the bed while Vic slept. It wasn't yet six in the morning. He hadn't slept long, but he had slept well, and he didn't want Noelle to wake and catch him in her mother's bed. Not yet. Not until they had a few things settled.

He dressed quickly, grabbed his cell phone from the end table and headed downstairs, dialing Shock's number as he went. Del woke his partner, and none of the news he got was good. As of four that morning, Holly had still been unconscious and the doctors said she might not make it. It wasn't the newer of her two wounds that threatened her life; knowing they'd need her alive Del had aimed for her shoulder. The old wound at her side had gone untended for too long, and that was the injury that could take her life at any moment.

More bad news. Preston was not at home in North Carolina or in his room at the hotel where he usually stayed when he was in Huntsville.

All this time, Vic had been worried about him bringing the danger of his job to Noelle, and it had been Preston mucking up the works. Only went to prove that danger could be anywhere and everywhere.

And no one could protect Noelle the way he could. No one.

Last night, Vic had again told him that she loved him. At least this time she'd been *awake*. But it was the moment talking, he figured. The passion of the moment and gratitude that he'd managed to bring Noelle home unharmed. He didn't want Vic to say she loved him because she was turned on, turned inside out or grateful. So what the hell did he want?

He wanted her to love him over pancakes, when he hogged the remote and when he forgot to pick his socks up off the floor. He wanted her to love him when she was irritated to no end by the little annoying habits she was sure to find he had.

Most of all, he wanted to love her back. He wanted to get rid of this lurking fear that if he loved Vic the way he once had, she'd break his heart again.

He was too damn old to be worried about a broken heart.

It was truly disgusting to watch the way the lovebirds acted when they thought no one was looking. For goodness' sake, they were in their thirties! They should know better.

Noelle walked into the kitchen, looking for a late breakfast, just as Wilder crept up behind her mother and wrapped his arms around her waist. Ugh, he was *kissing* her *neck*.

"Could you please show a little restraint?" Noelle asked, her voice suitably cool.

Her mother was a little embarrassed to be caught. Wilder was not. He just turned to Noelle and grinned. Did he have no shame?

"How do you feel this morning?" he asked.

"Fine." Her wrists ached a little, since they'd been bound so tight, and she'd had the most awful nightmares. But she wasn't going to stand here and complain. Most of all, she didn't want Wilder to know she had nightmares about him *not* showing up to save her. "I'll just make myself a bowl of cereal and take it to my room, and leave you two in private to…whatever." She shuddered dramatically as she made her way to the pantry.

When she came out of the small, narrow pantry, Lucky Charms in hand, she saw that Wilder was placing a bowl and spoon on the kitchen table and her mother was bringing over the milk from the refrigerator. Looked like she wouldn't be escaping to her room right away. Surely they weren't going to sit here and watch her eat!

She was almost grateful when Wilder's phone rang, and he stepped away. Noelle looked up from her seat at the table to find her mother too close, hovering and wringing her hands. So much had happened last night, they still hadn't discussed the newly discovered fact that Wilder was her biological father. It wasn't a conversation Noelle was anxious to have, mainly because she wasn't sure how she felt about this new development. She was still a little numb, and even though there were moments when she thought she liked Wilder, when she believed every word he said about love and staying and being a father who actually cared, deep inside she suspected that she might be better off without the guy in her life. He probably wouldn't be any better than her dad, in the long run.

Noelle couldn't let loose of the suspicion that Wilder was only being nice to her so he could nuzzle her mother's neck. Yew.

"I really am fine," she said, raising her eyebrows. "And I can't breathe when you stand that close."

Her mother backed up a step, but she didn't go away.

Wilder came back into the room, ending his conversation as he came toward the table. "Shock's on his way in."

Noelle's mom started to speak, but was interrupted by the doorbell.

"That's him." Wilder turned around to walk to the front of the house and answer the door.

"He called from the driveway?" Noelle mumbled. Probably didn't want to get shot by coming to the door unannounced.

"Got him," Shock said as he came into the kitchen. Wilder was right behind him.

Noelle's heart leaped. "The guy who hired that psycho bitch? You really caught him?"

"Noelle!" Her mother scolded. "Language."

Wilder didn't say anything, but he looked her in the eye and nodded his head in agreement. Geek.

Shock grabbed the box of cereal that sat in the middle of the table. "Hey, can I have a bowl? This is my favorite."

"Sure," Noelle said, annoyed that he was so easily distracted. "Did you really catch the guy?" She didn't want to have to wonder if there was someone else out there, just waiting to use her to get to Wilder. Being taped to a chair once was enough for a lifetime...and if she never had a gun pointed at her head again, it would be just fine with her. "He's, like, in jail?"

Shock cast a glance at Wilder, who responded with an almost imperceptible shake of his head. They were hiding things from her, Noelle knew it. But what?

"He's not exactly confessing, or anything like that, but he's in custody and that's where he'll stay, for a while."

"Who is he?" Noelle asked, taking a big spoonful of cereal into her mouth. "Some big-time drug dealer you two haven't been able to catch, or somebody Wilder just pissed off."

Her mother gave her that look again.

"Okay," Noelle said. "Somebody Wilder annoyed as much as he annoys me. Better?"

"Let's wait and make sure we have the right man before we start talking names," Wilder said, walking away to collect a bowl and spoon for his freaky partner.

Shock sat across from Noelle and poured his cereal. "My favorite lunch," he said in a confiding voice.

Noelle took a deep breath and continued eating. She was starved this morning. Her mother and Wilder poured fresh cups of coffee and stood close by, and Shock seemed to enjoy his cereal. She'd never before met a grown-up who actually liked Lucky Charms. Her mother always bought whole-grain crap with no sugar in it.

She liked Shock, more than she was ready to like Wilder, anyway. Shock wasn't good-looking, or tall, or normal in any way. Maybe that's why she liked him; she wasn't exactly normal, either.

"Do you have any other tattoos?" she asked between bites.

Shock shook his head. "Nope. Just the one." And then he cast a really quick glance toward Wilder.

Noelle smiled. They weren't going to get anything past her. "Does Wilder have a tattoo?"

"Well, yeah," Shock said.

Her bowl just about empty, Noelle pushed it away. "I wanna see."

"Nope," Wilder said. "Not today."

Noelle looked not at Wilder, but at Shock. "Is it, like, in some place really nasty where I *do not* want to look?"

Shock laughed, and Wilder supplied a quick "No."

"Why won't you show me? Oh, is the tattoo nasty?" This was really getting interesting. "Something...oh, my God, you have a tattoo of a naked woman somewhere on your body."

"No," both men said at about the same time.

Noelle glared at her fa— at Wilder. "Then why can't I see it?"

Shock waved his own spoon around. "Go ahead and let her see it, man. She's cool."

That's why she liked Shock. He thought she was cool.

Wilder looked like the kind of man who didn't change his mind very often, who didn't back down, who never surrendered. "Another time," he said.

Noelle stood, exasperated. "You know, you come in here, take over like you live here, drag me all over the place, get me shot at and kidnapped, turn out to be my…my sperm donor, expect me to *trust* you, and then when I ask for something really simple…"

"Fine," Wilder said sharply. "You can see the tattoo. But I have a condition." He held up one finger. "You never, ever again use the word *sperm*."

Noelle grinned. "Sure." That was a promise easily broken.

Wilder grabbed the tail end of his dark blue T-shirt and dragged it up. Noelle curled her lip. *This* sight she could do without. He stopped when the shirt had been lifted just far enough to reveal the tattoo on his chest.

Vic.

Her stomach constricted, just a little, but she didn't let her response show. There was something very sweet about that simple, faded tattoo. "Oh, my God," she said, no hint of emotion in her voice. "Mother, he mutilated himself for you. That's kind of disgusting." And kind of romantic, too, though she wouldn't say so out loud.

Wilder dropped his shirt. "Satisfied?"

"Not nearly," she said, leaving the room with her eyes straight ahead and her nose in the air.

Wilder said he loved her, but she couldn't make herself believe him, even now. He was going to find the bad guy, have his fun with Vic and then he'd be gone.

And sometimes she had a really bad feeling that no one would ever love her enough to mutilate himself for her.

As she climbed the stairs, she mumbled to herself. "Sperm, sperm, sperm."

A voice bellowed from the kitchen. "I heard that!"

She smiled as she closed the door to her room and fell onto the bed.

Chapter 15

Since his explosive return to Vic's life, they'd been on the run. In those days she'd dressed accordingly, sometimes in jeans and T-shirts, and even more often in those loose pantsuits she liked to wear. Comfortable and easy.

Today she wore a flowing dress, a pale blue background of gauzy fabric with a small pattern of flowers scattered here and there. It was feminine, it flowed around her legs when she walked...and that dress drove him crazy. Had she chosen it on purpose, just to plague him? Probably not. She had several dresses in the same style hanging in her closet. The dress was ultrafeminine, and her hair—loose and curling and hanging down her back—drove him every bit as wild as the dress.

Noelle's style was the antithesis of Vic's. Purposely? Probably. Try to dress her in anything that had flowers on it, and she'd surely rebel. Her hair was anything but long and flowing.

But then, she was his daughter as much as she was Vic's.

"You're kidding, right?" she asked as Del held the video in his hand up for her to see. "*Family day? I've been away from my friends forever, and you want me to stay here and watch movies with you?* Trust me, you two will have more fun without me." She rolled her eyes in disgust, to end the tirade.

"But it's my favorite movie," he said. He didn't want to argue that it still wasn't safe for her to be running around on her own, but he would if she left him no choice. It was bad enough that he'd left his Glock upstairs, along with his smaller six-shooter. Shock's Colt was in a lab in Birmingham, since it had been used to shoot Tripp Mayron during the raid on the cabin. Even though that was not the wound that had killed the man, the weapon would be out of commission for a while.

"Very funny, Wilder," Noelle said. "Mom told you that's my favorite movie, didn't she? What a lame gimmick."

"*Shrek* is your favorite movie, too?" he asked with a grin.

Vic jumped in. "I didn't tell him anything, Noelle. He came home with that video all on his own."

"Okay, fine," Noelle said sharply. "We'll watch *Shrek*. What are we going to do for the rest of the day? Play Scrabble?"

"I hope not," Del said. "I'm terrible at Scrabble."

She narrowed one eye. "Me, too. Whenever we play, Mom always kicks my…" She rolled her eyes again when Vic cleared her throat. "She always wins," she finished.

"We'll make cookies," Vic suggested.

Noelle was smarter than she usually let on. She knew

she couldn't leave the house unescorted, not until this thing was finished. If she was really smart, she didn't want to leave unescorted.

They hadn't told her that Preston was their prime suspect. Until they knew for sure, he didn't want to upset her with the news.

"They'd better be chocolate chip," she said darkly.

"Is there any other kind?" Del teased.

"After what I've been through, I *deserve* chocolate chip cookies."

Vic stood back. She watched, but she said nothing.

"Yes, you do," Del said, feeling so guilty the unexpected emotion sat in his stomach like a brick. "I'm so sorry that you got caught up in this."

"I'm not talking about the kidnapping, Wilder. I'm talking about finding out about *you.*"

"I'm going to go make a fresh pot of coffee," Vic said, inching toward the doorway.

Del cast Vic a pleading glance. She could step in here, make Noelle behave, make him behave. Her natural serenity was like a buffer between him and his daughter. Before Vic disappeared, she mouthed the words *You'll be fine.*

He wasn't so sure. "First of all," he said as Noelle plopped down onto the couch, "you're going to have to call me something besides Wilder. Like it or not I am your old man." He fidgeted a little. "You don't have to call me daddy, if you don't want to."

"Good," she muttered.

"But maybe you could call me Del, for now, or pops, or dad…"

"I have a Dad," she interrupted.

Not a very good one, but he kept that opinion to himself. "You don't have to make this so hard. I'm trying, I really am. I don't know what you want."

He expected an argument, or a terse explanation of what she *wanted*...which probably did not include a brand-new father...but Noelle remained silent. He almost liked her defiance better than this unnatural quiet.

"Vic tells me you play softball."

"What of it?"

"She also tells me you're pretty good."

"I guess."

"I used to play baseball. If you ever need any help with...anything..."

Noelle sighed tiredly, and Del felt like something on the bottom of her shoe. "What, are we supposed to bond today, or something? Is this, like, a belated father-daughter day?"

In spite of her outward contempt, her hard shell, Noelle was every bit as vulnerable as Vic. Del wanted to break Preston Lowell in half for doing this to them.

"I'm pushing too hard, aren't I?" he asked.

"Maybe."

"Fine," he said, losing what was left of his patience. "Forget it. Call me whatever you want. Give me the tough-girl attitude every day. Push as hard as you can, but I'm not going away, dammit."

"Language, Wilder," Noelle chastised, mocking her mother.

"No, you're not dancing out of this one with that smart mouth of yours." He leaned closer. No more mister nice guy, no more skirting around the issue. "Like it or not, I am your father. I'm not going anywhere, Noelle. You're not going to chase me away, no matter how hard you try."

Her face fell. "I don't imagine I'll need to," she said softly. "I imagine you'll run all on your own."

He leaned down until he was almost nose to nose. "I will never run," he seethed. "You're going to get so sick of me, kiddo, you might occasionally wish I'd run, but I won't. I might make a great softball coach. I will probably help you with your homework whether you want help or not. And I can't wait to meet this Chris of yours and let him know who's boss. I'll probably be a geek and embarrass you in front of your friends."

"Big surprise," she mumbled.

His frustration faded. "I have a lot of lost time to make up for, and if I make mistakes it's because I've never done this before."

"Chill, Wilder, you're just a…"

"Call me a sperm donor again and I'll ground you until you're thirty."

"You wouldn't dare."

Del turned away from Noelle, shoved the video into the VCR and returned to the couch to sit next to her. "Try me," he said.

As the movie began he added, "And let's work on the daddy thing. It's just not right for a girl to call her father by his last name."

"I'll think about it."

That was all he could ask, for now.

Since she'd heard Del enter the kitchen, she wasn't surprised when he slipped his arms around her waist.

"Smells good," he said.

Vic continued to move the warm cookies from the pan to the cooling rack. "This is our ritual for hard times."

"Cookies?"

"Homemade cookies," she clarified. "Though to be

honest, we have resorted to a bag of Oreos, on occasion."

"That's not right," he said, touching her neck with his mouth. "Surely you make cookies in happy times, too."

"Yes, but…" She didn't want to talk to Del about hard times and good ones long past. She wanted to talk about now. "What's Noelle doing?"

"Watching the movie again. Anything to keep from talking to me, I guess." He sighed and drew her close. "This is hard, Vic."

"Being a father?"

"Yeah. What if I never do anything right?"

She smiled. "You will."

He hummed and kissed her neck again. "Noelle is…difficult. I can never tell what she's thinking. One minute it looks like everything's going to be fine, the next I'm sure she hates me."

"You think this is difficult? You should have been around when she was two."

Del didn't answer, and in a heartrending second Vic knew why. He'd missed two. He'd missed fourteen. He'd missed everything.

"You look so good in that dress," he said, changing the subject. "And you smell like cookies. I could eat you up, here and now." His hand skimmed to cup one breast. "I can start right here." He moved her hair aside so he could kiss her neck properly, tongue and lips dancing over her sensitive flesh. "I don't suppose we could make a quick trip into the pantry."

"We'd better not," she said. "Tonight."

"That's hours away," he complained.

The sex was easy with them. Powerful, beautiful…but uncomplicated. Nothing else between them was so easy.

If this was going to last, they had to have more than the physical.

"You know," she said, no more anxious to delve into uncomfortable subjects than Del was, "you never did get me a gun."

"Not that again," he moaned.

"Well, it is unfinished business."

Del tried to distract her with his mouth again, kissing her neck. "When we find the chance to get to a firing range and get you properly trained, then maybe we'll get you a little pistol or a small six-shooter."

"Maybe?" she turned in his arms and smiled up at him. "Why are you so determined that I not get a gun?"

"You don't need one."

"I don't?"

"You have me." He tried to end the argument with a kiss, but when the kiss was over she continued.

"Are you really afraid I'll shoot myself in the foot?"

He took her hands in his and looked down at them, kissing each palm—one and then the other. "These hands are made for better things, Vic. They're made for holding babies and painting beautiful pictures and touching me. I have enough of guns and violence in my life. You're…you're…"

"I'm what?" she whispered when he froze.

"You and Noelle are the better part of my life. The best part. I don't want to see you with a gun in your hand because I…because I brought that violence into your life."

"But if it was Preston who did this, you didn't bring trouble to us…we brought it to you."

"Doesn't matter. It's still a part of my world. Not yours."

She didn't like that separation of worlds. They should

be living in the same world, now and forever. If he brought some of his with him, so be it. She'd make up for that by bringing love and peace to his world.

"I can teach you how to fight, though," he said in compromise.

"Oh, you can."

He moved back, one step. "It never hurts to know a little bit about self-defense. There are quite a few sensitive areas where a single blow can give you time to run."

"Run?" she asked, smiling.

"Run," he said, perfectly serious. "The first thing most women think of is to go for the testicles, and that's okay, but most men are looking for that. So while he's protecting the family jewels, you go for the eyes or deliver a hard blow to the nose. The flat of your hand is best. If you can't get a good shot at the face, whack him hard in the throat. You can always go for the kidneys, or grab on tight and pull back a finger until you hear it pop."

"Yew," Vic said, sounding very much like Noelle.

Del's jaw tensed. "You don't want to break a finger, but you think shooting someone would be okay."

"It's not that," Vic complained.

"You think it's more distant, safer somehow, to pull a trigger?" His eyes were dark, and he showed her, momentarily, a Del Wilder she didn't know. The DEA agent, the man who was accustomed to facing violence every day. "It's not. A firearm is up close and very, very personal." He moved back in, close once again. "If the idea of breaking a finger repels you, you won't pull the trigger...and then that gun you want so badly instantly becomes a weapon that can be used against you."

She rested her head on his chest. Maybe he was right. "So I should stick to curling irons for defense."

"You should let me take care of you."

When he said that it sounded so permanent. So wonderfully permanent. "Okay."

"You two need a chaperon more than any couple I know."

Del and Vic separated as Noelle entered the kitchen.

"Can I have some cookies without being forced to watch this—"

"If you call me middle-aged again," Del interrupted, "you're grounded."

Noelle rolled her eyes. "Is that your answer for everything?" She actually smiled. A little. She grabbed a handful of warm cookies and glanced around the messy kitchen. "Whenever Mom cooks, the kitchen ends up looking like a bag of groceries exploded."

"Me?" Vic responded. "When you made pizza for your friends, it took me days to clean up all the sauce." She looked at Del. "It was everywhere. Just when I thought I had it all, I'd run across another drop or two. I swear, there was sauce on the floor of the pantry."

"It was my first time," Noelle explained. "And the pizza *was* good."

"You cook!" Del said with a widening grin. "That's so domestic. I never would have thought it of you. Make me a pizza sometime?"

Noelle looked like she was about to refuse, but after a second thought she finally said, "Sure." She took her cookies and returned to the movie.

Del took Vic in his arms again. "I don't know if that's a good sign or if I should hire a food taster."

"It's a good sign," Vic assured him.

* * *

It was almost dark outside…but gray hung in the sky and drifted through the windows.

He found Vic in the upstairs hallway, putting away the laundry she'd done that afternoon. She'd dropped a few of Noelle's things onto the bed in the girl's room and had a small stack of her own clothes in her hands.

She glanced over her shoulder. "Did I hear Shock downstairs?"

"Yeah."

"Any news?"

"Nothing from Preston, but Holly's doing better. Looks like she's going to make it."

Her face went pale. "Has she identified Preston as the man who hired her?"

He shook his head. "No. She's still doped up and unable to do that, but she's going to make it. When we go to trial, she'll be able to testify."

Vic walked into the bedroom and placed her clothes on the dresser. "Will she?"

"Testify against the man who killed Tripp? Without question."

She sighed in relief. "Good." She headed for the master bath, grabbed a washcloth and, after wetting it slightly, held it to her face.

"Are you okay?" He followed her into the small room.

Her hands trembled a little, and she tried to hide that response from him by clenching her hands into tight fists. "Yeah, it's just…I lived with Preston for years. I never loved him, and he knew that. Maybe there were times when I tried to like him, and maybe on his good days I succeeded. Most of the time he was just a lousy husband and father."

"I know." He pulled her close, tried to comfort her. This close, he felt the trembling she tried to hide.

"I never thought that he might be a…a killer. Why didn't I see that?" She pressed her cheek to his chest. "Am I such a poor judge of character that I can't see evil in a man I *lived* with?"

Del picked her up and placed her on the vanity, so they were face-to-face. "No," he said. "Evil doesn't come with a neon sign. It hides. It waits. We never see evil until it's too late."

And sometimes we don't see good until it slaps us in the face.

"I'm not leaving," he said softly, his mind made up. "Not this time. Noelle can call me middle-aged and geek and she can tell me she doesn't want me as her father, but I'm not leaving."

Vic smiled and stroked his cheek. "I know. No matter what Noelle says, she needs you. If she fights it's because she doesn't know what to do with a father who loves her."

He moved forward slightly. Vic's thighs parted so he fit between them. "I'm not staying just for Noelle."

"You don't…"

"I would," he said. "If there was nothing else for me here, if there was only Noelle…I'd stay. But there's more here, isn't there?"

"Yes," she whispered as his hands skimmed over her bare legs, pushing her skirt toward her waist.

Without turning around, he kicked the door shut. Quietly.

Vic smiled at him. "Where's Noelle?"

"She and Shock are eating Lucky Charms and discussing the finer plot points of *Shrek*."

"Good." She cradled his head and kissed him, so

sweet and sexy that he melted inside while his body grew hard.

Vic kissed him as if she were hungry, as if she were starving for him. Only him. Those hands he loved—artist's hands, lover's hands—caressed him gently. One of those hands slipped beneath his shirt and rested over his heart for a moment before circling around to lie against his back.

"I can't ever get enough of you," he said as he slipped her panties off and down and tossed them aside.

She responded with a satisfied hum as she wrapped her legs around him.

He touched her, teased her, while she perched on the vanity before him. Vic, so open and honest, let her head fall back as she moaned, low in her throat and so very intoxicating. Her body quivered against him as he leaned into her to kiss that long, bared throat.

Her fingers trembled as she unfastened his belt buckle, as she lowered his zipper and freed his erection. Those trembling fingers caressed him, long and slow, then harder, while he brought his mouth to hers.

Vic wrapped her legs tighter around his hips while she guided him into her waiting, tight warmth.

He entered her slowly, pushing deep. Making himself a part of her, and realizing that Vic was as much inside him as he was inside her.

In the tiny bathroom, Vic perched before him and hanging on tight, he made love to her without restraint. Hard and fast, he filled her, stroked her. They had made love before, slow and fast, hard and gentle. This…this was different. It was primal, and intimate in a way he had never experienced before. He claimed her; she took him in. She claimed him; he gave her everything he had.

She pulsed around him, came with a low, deep cry while her body shuddered around his.

Satisfied, Vic rested her head on his shoulder and sighed. Neither of them said a word, they just held on and tried to breathe.

Del raked his hand down her back, kissed her neck, refused to let go.

She was his, and he was home.

Chapter 16

With Preston in custody, the manpower out front had been downgraded. The surveillance detail had been cut down to two locals once again, and Del had had to beg to keep those two on duty for another few hours. His logic in coming up with Preston as his main suspect was too clear to ignore. Still, he wanted Lowell to confess, he wanted Holly to wake up and identify Preston as *Bob*. Until then, he wasn't going to rest.

It was night again. Noelle was sleeping, had gone to bed early claiming—in a long-suffering voice—that there was nothing to do. In truth, the kid was exhausted. She might not admit it, but Del had seen it. He'd wanted to climb the stairs with her and tuck her in. He hadn't even tried.

It had been a good day where Noelle was concerned; at least, he thought so. Maybe she was a little less angry than she'd been last night and this morning. Maybe she hadn't glared at him quite so audaciously, as the day went on. Still, he didn't think she was ready for him to run up the stairs and tuck her in. Fifteen was probably too old for such nonsense, and Noelle was certainly too cool for something so lame.

But he would check on her, after she was sound asleep and couldn't protest.

Vic was restless, and had been all day. Their coming together early in the evening had done nothing to ease her nervousness. In fact, she had been more jumpy than before, as she'd straightened her pretty blue dress and tried to make herself look like she hadn't just been well loved.

Something was on her mind, but she wasn't letting him in on whatever bothered her. She paced, she studied her fingernails as if she expected to find something there, and she jumped out of her skin at the slightest sound.

As for him, he just wanted this to be over. He wanted the danger past so he could get on with his life, whatever that might mean. Changes. If nothing else, he knew his life was about to change.

His Glock sat on the table by the couch, handy in case he should need it. He'd gone upstairs to collect it after Noelle had gone to bed. What did it say about him that he felt better with a weapon within reach, always?

Vic quit pacing and sat next to him on the couch. The television played before them, the volume low. He hadn't been paying attention to the sitcom rerun, and neither had Vic. Moving slowly, she reached over and took his hand. Her fingers threaded through his as she leaned into his side, cuddling against him. In spite of everything that had happened since his return, in spite of the bumps in the road and the uncertainty that still plagued him, it was nice.

"How about now," she said softly.

"What?"

"How about if I tell you I love you now," she said, not looking up, but grasping his hand more tightly. "My heart is perfectly calm," she added. "I'm breathing very well, and we're both completely dressed."

"Vic..."

"Never mind," she said. "I wanted to tell you this evening, I had to bite back the words. You accused me of only being brave enough to say those words when we make love. That's when it's easiest, I guess. That's when I want to shout out the words I kept buried for so long. I love you, Del. I love you more than you will ever know."

He knew he belonged here, he knew he would never let Vic or Noelle go...so why did the words stick in his throat?

"Maybe you don't want me to love you," Vic said when the time for him to say "I love you, too" had come and gone. "Maybe it's just too soon or too fast, or maybe you still haven't forgiven me, but, Del—" She lifted her face, looked him dead in the eye. "It's not going to go away. It never did."

Del tipped his face down and kissed her, soft and brief. He wanted more. He wanted everything. "Nothing scares me anymore," he whispered. "At least, nothing scared me until I came here and found...this."

"I scare you?"

"The way you make me feel, that scares me." He knew what she wanted, what she needed. He just wasn't sure he could give it to her. In the end, would it all turn ugly again?

"How do you feel?"

Like you're inside me, all the time. Like I belong here.

Like when I walked through that front door, I was coming home. "Confused."

She sighed and settled back against his side. "I know what you mean."

Del tried his own vow in the recesses of his mind. Vic was right; it would be easiest to make love to her, and make the confession while he was inside her. Control gone, passion flaring...*I love you* seemed perfectly reasonable, perfectly right.

But sitting on the couch holding hands, thinking about the future and the past, saying the words was harder.

The doorbell rang, surprising them both. Vic jumped a little, but she rose quickly to answer the door.

"I'll get it," Del said, wondering why the guys out front hadn't called in to let him know who was at the door. Rookies, probably.

"I can answer the door, Del," Vic said as she walked past him.

He grabbed his Glock from the table and stuck it at his spine, where it would be handy but out of sight, and was right behind Vic when she peered through the peephole in her front door. She glanced over her shoulder. "It's Ryan Parrish," she said, wrinkling her nose. "I'll get rid of him quick."

He hadn't yet met Parrish, but no one Vic had dated was on his list of people he'd most like to socialize with. Especially now.

Parrish was facing the street, waving to the cops who sat in the unmarked car at the curb. They waved back and hefted bottles of soda in their hands. Morons.

Parrish turned around slowly, away from Del at first, his head down as he stepped into the foyer and reached back to close the door behind him.

When the man lifted his head, Del reached for his gun.

"Don't try it," Robert Parvin said, his own gun popping up and taking aim at Vic. He cocked his head and smiled. "Surprised to see me?"

He hadn't seen Parvin for three years. "I thought you were dead."

"That was the plan." Parvin glanced toward the stairwell. "Is the kid asleep?"

Vic glanced from Del to Parvin. "What's going on?"

The man she'd called Ryan Parrish poked her in the ribs with the gun. "Is she asleep?" he asked again.

"Yes."

Parvin gestured toward Del with the gun. "Drop your weapon slowly, Wilder. Easy. Two fingers only. We don't want to wake Noelle up. There's no reason to involve her in this." He smiled. "Not yet, anyway."

Del very easily drew his Glock, using two fingers as Parvin had instructed. He dipped down and placed the gun on the floor.

Again, Parvin glanced toward the stairs. "Let's move into the living room."

They did, Vic trembling as she looked from Del to her father's friend and back again. "Who is he?"

"Robert Parvin. I never knew him as Bob, but I do remember him using the name Bobby Joe at one time. He's a gun runner, or at least he was last time I checked. He disappeared years ago. Word was, and still is, that he was executed and buried in a slab of concrete somewhere."

"Yes," Parvin said. "All true. Well, except for the part about me being dead. I always found guns more profitable than other ventures, but my little sister was into drugs. That's how she got acquainted with Agent Wilder. He sent her to jail." His face hardened. "She died there, did you know that?"

"Yes, I heard," Del said softly. "I'm sorry, that wasn't..."

Parvin whipped out his free hand and slapped Vic across the cheek. Hard. Del took a step forward, but was stopped when the weapon Parvin held was once again aimed at Vic's head.

"You annoy me, she pays," Parvin said tightly. "Is that clear?"

"Yes," Del whispered. An unexpected helplessness welled up inside him. The sight of that gun at Vic's head made him literally ill, and there was nothing he could do until Parvin moved the threat away from her. "You won't get away with this," he said. "The police out front, they saw you come in."

"Don't worry about them. They're nice young men. I met them last night, outside Archard's house. Took them a little something to eat, before your unfortunate return. They'll be out cold in a few minutes, and by the time they wake up, this will all be over."

"What are you going to do?" Vic asked.

Parvin looked at her and smiled. "Preston will be here soon."

"Preston is in jail," Del said.

The armed man cocked his head to one side. "Not anymore. I have a very good attorney, and you have no evidence that Preston is behind recent unfortunate events. Not yet, anyway," Parvin added.

"What do you want?" Del asked softly.

"I want you dead, I want Victoria dead, I want Preston to take the fall..." Parvin leaned in and smiled. "And I want your little girl."

Del's fingers itched. If he was fast enough, sure enough...no, not like this. Not when his blood was boiling. He'd get them all killed, that way. If only the gun would drop, just a little, so it wasn't aimed so damned surely at Vic's head.

"You've been planning this a long time," Del said casually.

"Three years, since the day I buried my sister." He gestured with the barrel of the gun. "She mentioned the tattoo, once. *Vic.* Took me two years and four private investigators to trace your background and connect you to Victoria." He grinned. "The first time I saw Noelle, I knew she was your kid. It was more than the hair and the eyes that convinced me. She's a pain in the ass, just like you are. A real little firecracker."

"You leave her out of this."

Parvin shook his head. "No can do. In a couple of years I'll marry her off to my little brother, Ricky, I'll become the solid, dependable father figure and we'll be one, big, happy family."

"What makes you think she'll have anything to do with you or your brother?" Del asked in a reasonably calm voice. "If I remember correctly, Ricky has a bigger drug problem than Celeste did. I can't see women exactly breaking down his door with marriage in mind."

Parvin was not dissuaded. "If you drug a woman enough, she'll do anything you tell her to. Anything at all."

"You stay away from my daughter," Del said darkly.

"You're in no position to issue orders," Parvin said smugly.

He couldn't rush Parvin, not with the gun pointed at Vic's head. The two cops outside were unconscious, or soon would be. Help was not on the way, not tonight.

"You haven't thought this through," Del said. "You gave the cops cold drinks that have been drugged. You think they won't remember that?"

"I told them my good friend Preston Lowell asked me to drop those off, and to be on the lookout since Lowell would be along shortly. Since I had Preston hand me those bottles yesterday, his fingerprints are on them. With all the other evidence against him..." Parvin shrugged. "It'll do."

"All because I did my job." Del shook his head. "I'm sorry Celeste is dead. She was a good kid. Messed up, yeah, but with a little help she should have been fine. You..." Del pointed at Parvin. "You should be sorry you dragged her into a world she wasn't prepared for."

"I could have taken care of her if you hadn't sent her to jail."

"You had your chance to take care of her, and you blew it," Del accused. "You introduced her to drug dealers who got her hooked and used her and made her run their dirty errands. Jail had to be an improvement over the life you provided for your little sister."

Parvin grinned. "I know what you're trying to do, Wilder. Make me mad enough and I'll lose my cool, maybe make a move before Preston gets here. That would give you a chance to play the hero." He moved the muzzle of his weapon down to Vic's throat, pressed it against the soft flesh there. "I'm not playing."

Vic's eyes met his. She hadn't said a word, was frozen to the spot in terror. And there was nothing he could do. Not yet.

"I wanted this one, just for fun," Parvin continued, raking the muzzle down the side of Vic's neck. "I thought it would be amusing to seduce the mother of your child. I had such great plans for her." He tsked. "But she'd have none of me, cold bitch that she is. Of course, the night is young."

"Touch her and I'll kill you."

"Big talk for a man with no gun, no backup... nowhere to go."

"I will kill you," Del said again.

"I don't think so," Parvin answered, unconcerned.

"All this because I sent Celeste to jail?" Del was gradually losing what little cool he had left. "It doesn't make any sense!"

"You slept with her and then sent her to prison! You broke her heart and made her...she didn't care if she lived or died, so when she got sick she just wasted away."

"I did not sleep with your sister!" Del argued.

Parvin shook his head. "Then how did she know about the tattoo?"

It took him a moment, but he finally remembered. "I got caught in the rain one night," Del said. "I changed my shirt in that bar where she hung out. That's all."

Parvin was not satisfied. "Then why did she love you?" he shouted.

"I don't know," Del said softly. "I had no idea."

Vic licked her lips, her hands trembled. Del tried to tell her, with a meeting of their eyes and a gentle nod of his head, that everything would be fine. He didn't know how, but somehow he had to make everything all right.

"After Celeste went to jail and I found out you were responsible, I told her I would kill you for what you'd done. She begged me not to." Parvin shook his head in wonder.

Del wanted to charge forward, but Parvin held the gun pointed at Vic. He had to do something, and soon.

"Gunshots will wake Noelle," he said. "Do you really think she'll have anything to do with you after this?

She's gonna know what you did. Drugs or no drugs, she'll never accept you as a father figure."

"That's why we're waiting for Preston," Parvin explained. "It's going to happen very fast. Three gunshots, a matter of seconds. By the time Noelle gets down here, it'll be over. I'll be forced to shoot Preston and save Noelle, of course." He smiled again. "Every girl loves a hero."

Del's heart hammered. There was no reasoning with a man like Parvin...he wasn't going to talk his way out of this one.

"Don't point that at Vic," he said, unable to help himself.

Parvin grinned. "Hurts, doesn't it?" He touched the muzzle of his weapon to Vic's hair, lifting a honey-colored curl and twirling it around the barrel.

Hell, yes, it hurt.

The doorbell rang.

Noelle tried to cover her head with the pillow. The doorbell, again! What were the lovebirds doing down there, having a party?

A voice she knew drifted to her room, through the closed door and to her sharp ears. Her dad's voice had a way of carrying, like a little dog's yap.

Noelle sat up. For years, she'd hoped that her parents would get back together. Maybe then her father would be happy enough to smile now and then, her mother would have something to do besides be psycho super-mom and she...she could be normal.

That wasn't going to happen, she knew that now. But wouldn't it be fun to watch Wilder sweat?

Her wicked smile faded. Wilder had tried today, hadn't he? Okay, maybe he tried too hard, but that was better than not trying at all. Softball coach, help with her homework, meeting all her friends!

That was all gross, but how cool would it be when everyone found out that her real father had a tattoo *and* an earring? She called Wilder a dweeb now and then, but he was really kind of cool for a middle-aged guy.

Noelle left the bed quietly. Her pajamas were perfectly decent, even if someone besides the lovebirds and her dad were down there. They were baggy and black, some kind of fake silk stuff. The pants were a little bit too long, and so were the sleeves.

She slipped down the stairs, listening to voices in the living room.

"What the hell are you doing?" her dad…the man she had always thought was her dad…asked.

She knew the voice that answered, had met the man a few times. A friend of Grandpa's, Ryan something. He'd dated her mom a couple of times. "Don't be an idiot, Preston."

Noelle went still on the stairs.

Wilder spoke up. "There's no reason not to let Vic and Noelle go. Let them walk out of here right now and we can settle this between us."

"You should let me go, too," her dad said frantically. "I don't have anything to do with this, whatever it is."

"Shut up, Preston," Wilder said sharply. "Let me get the kid out of here," he said, his voice a strange, forced calm. "You don't want her to wake up and find you here. Let Vic and Noelle…"

"No!" Ryan answered. "You idiot, killing you is not going to be enough. If it was, I could have done away with you months ago, I could have stepped up to you as you were going home one night and blown a bullet through your skull. The woman and the kid, they're part of your payback." There was a moment of strained silence. "You know, I thought the original plan was clever. I figured Victoria would tell you, before the bomb went off, that you had a child you would never see. With you two dead, I'd pin the thing on Lowell and proceed with my plan. But this is so much better. You get to know how and why before you die. Makes me almost happy that those two morons screwed up and let you escape."

"I'm begging you," Wilder said in a low voice that cut to the bone. "Let Vic and Noelle go. This doesn't have anything to do with them. It's just you and me, Parvin. I'll do anything."

"I told you," her dad...Preston Lowell said again. "I'm not a part of this. Let me go and I swear I won't tell anyone...."

"Sit down and shut up!" Ryan ordered.

Noelle lowered herself to the steps, her knees shaking. For the first time, it occurred to her that it wasn't her fault the man she'd thought was her dad didn't love her. Her friend Melanie was adopted and her dad was great! Her own dad was just...a selfish jerk. She was glad he wasn't her real father. He would never beg for anyone but himself.

Sitting here wasn't going to help matters any. She very quietly climbed the stairs, crept into her mother's room and went to the phone. If she dialed 911 and the police came with lights and sirens, would Ryan what's-his-name...Parvin. Wilder had called him Parvin... would he panic and shoot everyone? She scrolled through the caller ID until she came to the Birmingham cell phone number, then punched the numbers into the phone.

A comforting voice answered the phone.

"Shock?" she whispered.

*   *   *

Vic watched as the man she'd known as Ryan Parrish for the past year swung the weapon away from her head and took aim at Del. She could see the relief wash over Del's face as the danger switched to him. She knew what he was thinking, could read his intentions too well. He was going to rush Parvin, try to wrest the gun away, and he was going to get himself shot in the process.

"Hello?" a sleepy voice called from the stairwell. "What are y'all doing down here? I'm trying to sleep."

Parvin moved close to Vic and pointed the gun at her ribs. From this angle, Noelle wouldn't be able to see the weapon. "Get rid of her," he whispered. "Send her back to bed." He glanced at Del. "Make a move and I'll shoot them both." He didn't have to worry about Preston, who was obediently sitting on the sofa, his spine straight and his face paper white.

Noelle came into the room yawning, her baggy pajamas making her look younger than fifteen, her strangely red hair sticking out at all angles.

"What is this, a party?" She blinked and looked at all three men. "Mother," she said coolly. "One date at a time. Even I know that."

"This is just…business, sweetheart," Vic said. "You get back to bed. It's been a long day." She didn't want Parvin to get his hands on Noelle, ever. Right now she had to trust that Del would get them out of this somehow, that Parvin would never have a chance to get close to their daughter.

"I had a bad dream," Noelle said, heading for Del, her feet shuffling, the hem of her pajama bottoms dragging across the carpet. "I had a dream that Wilder didn't show up." Her lower lip trembled, just a little. "And that psycho bitch shot everybody. I *hate* having bad dreams.''

"Me, too, baby," Del said as Noelle walked into his arms.

Noelle wrapped her arms around Del's waist and buried her head against his chest. Del placed one big hand against unnatural red hair, the other at Noelle's back.

Preston stood. "I'll walk you up to bed, Noelle," he said, apparently seeing a chance for escape. "Come along."

"Sit down, Preston," Parvin said firmly.

Preston complied quickly.

Vic stared at the way Noelle held on to Del, her arms around his waist, her cheek pressed to his chest, her eyes closed. When had Noelle become so sentimental? So emotional? She really must have had a bad dream.

Then again, Noelle and Del were so much alike, they would probably become close very quickly. If they got the chance.

"Very touching," Parvin whispered in her ear. "Get rid of the kid now or I'll shoot them both where they stand." The muzzle of the gun pressed more insistently against a rib.

"Noelle," Vic said sharply. "We really do have business to discuss. You run on up to bed."

Noelle disengaged herself from Del slowly, as if she really didn't want to let him go. This was so unfair. They hadn't had a chance.

Noelle stepped away from Del, but she didn't leave the room. She stopped, crossed her arms over her chest, and glared at Parvin. "You're Ryan, right? Grandpa's friend? I have to warn you, you're standing too close to my mother. Wilder here has a *very* jealous streak, and I wouldn't want to get on his bad side, if you know what I mean.''

"I'll take that into consideration." Parvin actually did take a step back, but stood behind Vic so that the gun remained pointed at her and Noelle would still not be able to see the weapon.

If Parvin wanted to marry Noelle off in a few years, he wouldn't want to alienate her now. And if he ordered her from the room, she'd remember that when everyone in the room but him ended up dead. He had to be the good guy, the smiling, agreeable victim who would save her...in a few minutes or a few hours.

Vic took a nice long blink, letting her eyes remain closed for a couple of seconds. She trusted Del, she loved him, and she knew he would get them out of this if he could. She only wished she could read his mind, so she'd know what he wanted her to do.

"It's okay, kiddo," Del said calmly. "You go on to bed. I'll check on you later and make sure there are no more bad dreams."

Noelle didn't smile, but she did nod and shuffle from the room. At the archway between the foyer and the living room, she looked back at the man seated on the couch. "Oh, yeah. Good night, Dad."

Preston muttered a coldly disinterested good-night, and Noelle disappeared. She didn't immediately go upstairs but padded into the kitchen. A cupboard opened, the faucet ran for a moment. They all listened as Noelle got herself a drink of water and then climbed the stairs. The door to her room above opened and closed.

"It's not going to work," Del said, his voice low. "Walk away now, while you can."

Parvin shook his head. "No. If things don't go well and I have to kill you all, Noelle included, so be it. Ryan

Parrish can disappear in a heartbeat, and no one will ever be able to find him.'' He smiled crookedly. ''But trust me, Wilder, if I have to kill the girl tonight, it won't be quick and it won't be easy. I was planning to wait a few years, before stepping in to relieve Ricky of a husband's duties, but if tonight is the night…I'll bet she's not as meek and cold as this one.'' With the hand that didn't hold a weapon, he caressed Vic's cheek.

''No,'' she said, seeing red as her blood pounded harder and harder. This man was not going to touch her little girl. She had not spent years protecting her child just so someone like Parvin could come along and harm her. She planted her feet, her elbow swinging up and directly into his gut. Surprised, Parvin yelped. The weapon he held swung to the side, and she turned and swung at his face with the heel of her hand, striking him in the nose.

Parvin recovered quickly, angry and hurting, and he raised his weapon again.

Del stepped forward, one hand reaching behind his back, and Parvin's target changed in a heartbeat to cover the threat. As Parvin took aim at Del, Vic rushed at him and knocked his gun arm to the side. The weapon discharged as it swung away. Preston cried out, and Del ran forward, placing himself between her and Parvin.

Del had a small gun in his hand, a weapon she knew he hadn't had tucked at his spine when Parvin had arrived. He kicked the gun out of Parvin's hand, and the weapon went flying. It landed on a table by the window and knocked a vase of flowers down. The vase cracked and rolled to the floor.

Del held the muzzle of the revolver he sometimes carried in his boot pressed to Parvin's forehead. The muscles in Del's jaw twitched, his neck was corded with tension. "Give me an excuse," he said softly. "Breathe the wrong way so I can shoot you." Parvin didn't move.

"He shot me," Preston whined.

Vic glanced at her ex-husband. He had one hand pressed against his thigh. A trickle of blood marred his pants.

Noelle came running down the stairs, called, no doubt, by the gunfire. "Daddy!" she cried before she reached the entryway. She came to an abrupt halt in the archway, and her eyes landed on a moaning Preston.

A new expression flitted over Del's face. Pain. Not physical pain, but the pain of hearing his daughter call another man Daddy.

"Daddy?" Noelle said again, and this time her eyes went to Del. "It worked?"

Del grinned. "Sure did. Call the police."

"I already called Shock," she said, staying in the foyer and well away from Parvin. "He should be here any minute."

"I'm here," a voice called, and Shock sidled up beside Noelle, gun in hand. He'd apparently come in through the back door without making a sound. "And it looks like I missed all the fun. Again." He grinned at Noelle. "Thanks for unlocking the kitchen door for me, kid."

"No problem."

Del and Shock handcuffed Parvin, and Vic went to her daughter. "Are you okay?" she asked, hands on her daughter's soft face.

"I'm fine."

"What did you do?" Vic asked, taking hold of Noelle's arm and holding on tight. "Did you...slip Del a gun?"

Noelle grinned widely. "Yeah. I went into your room

to call Shock, and I saw the gun on the dresser and—'' she shrugged ''—seemed like the thing to do.''

"She's good," Del said as he left a wounded Preston and a handcuffed Parvin to Shock. Through the curtains, blue flashing lights broke the night.

Del's smile was soft and real. "My first hug from my daughter and it's a ploy to slip me a weapon."

"Complaining, Wilder?"

His smile faded, just a little. "No way. I kinda like the daddy part," he said softly.

Noelle blushed. "Don't get used to it. I was caught up in the moment."

"I've been shot!" Preston complained to Shock.

Shock was not impressed. "That? That's just a scratch. You'll live."

"Victoria!" Preston called. "Help me!"

Del opened the door for the police, and then the three of them stepped into the kitchen while the uniformed officers, who had already spoken to Shock by phone, took custody of Parvin and took charge of a moaning Preston.

"We just have a few minutes," Del said, his voice low and quick. "It'll take me all night to get this straightened out, and dammit, I can't wait all night for this." He grabbed Noelle and hugged her. "You're brave and beautiful and...and if you ever touch one of my guns again, you're grounded."

Noelle laughed lightly and hugged him back. "Gee, Wilder, you're tough to please."

"And I really do like the daddy thing. I know you said it was a 'moment' thing, but maybe we can work on that a little?"

"Sure...Daddy."

Del kissed Noelle on the forehead and turned to Vic.

No matter what happened between the two of them, Del was going to be a great father to Noelle. He was going to make up for all the indifference Preston had shown her.

Del took Vic's face in his hand and kissed her on the lips, long and hard and slow. It was a good kiss.

"Gross," Noelle said, and she started to leave the room.

Without taking his eyes from Vic, Del ordered Noelle to wait. Amazingly, she obeyed. She stopped in the doorway and leaned there, waiting.

Del dropped down to one knee. "Marry me, Vic."

Vic shook her head. She wouldn't marry Del just so he could be with Noelle, no matter how much she wanted to say yes, no matter what his reason for asking. "You don't have to marry me. You can see Noelle anytime. You can stay here, you can—"

"I love you," Del said, his eyes on her face as he knelt before her. "I want to be here every morning, I want to be a husband to you and a father to Noelle. We're family. We became family the minute I saw you at the warehouse and I'm not giving you up. Not ever again."

She wanted to believe him, she really did. But there was a niggling doubt.... "Maybe we should think it over for a few days."

"Mom!" Noelle protested. "What's wrong with you? Say yes!"

Vic reached down and brushed at Del's hair, her fingers tender. "It's too fast."

"Too fast! I'd say I'm sixteen freakin' years late!"

Noelle giggled. "Daddy!"

"Sorry," Del mumbled. He didn't get up.

"Cops are coming this way," Noelle said, turning around. "I'll keep them occupied for a few minutes."

"I can tell you everything!" she said as she walked toward the officers. "It was really, really *scary*." Her voice faded as she led the police away from the kitchen.

"Stand up," Vic said, brushing her fingers across Del's cheek.

"I love you," he said again, staying on his knees. "Why won't you believe me?"

"Tomorrow morning, when the adrenaline rush is over, you'll come to your senses. I don't want you to regret asking me to marry you in the heat of the moment. Maybe this thing you're feeling isn't really love, it's just relief and…and lust."

Del didn't move. "Dammit, Vic, you make everything difficult."

"Why now?" she whispered. "Why not before Ryan…Parvin…whoever he is…showed up? Tomorrow morning, when everything's a little calmer and you're thinking straight, we'll talk again."

"I don't want to wait until tomorrow morning!"

"Del, please."

He took a deep breath and looked into her eyes. "You said you were angry at me for not believing, sixteen years ago, that you loved me. You said I should have been able to look into your eyes and see the love.

"Look at me, Vic," he whispered. "Look at me and tell me that I don't love you."

She did. She looked deep into his eyes and saw not adrenaline, not lust, but love. For her and for Noelle. It had been there for a while…it had been there this afternoon when they'd made love, while they'd been sitting on the couch holding hands, days ago, when he'd been angry and confused…the love had always been there.

Vic dropped to her knees to lay her hands on his face. "I love you," she whispered.

"Marry me."

"Yes."

He kissed her, long and deep, while they knelt face-to-face. She didn't want to ever let him go, but she was going to have to. Soon.

When he took his mouth from hers, he grinned. "I don't have a ring."

"That's okay...."

"No, it's not." He removed his earring, placed it on her palm and closed her fingers over it. "This will do for now."

Noelle came running back into the kitchen. "They want to talk to Wilder, and I can't keep them back anymore. Are we getting married?" she asked breathlessly.

Vic and Del turned their heads to smile at their daughter, and for the first time in her entire life, Vic felt as if her life was complete.

"Yes."

Epilogue

Sweet sixteen and Christmas Eve. Del had insisted that there be no Christmas theme or talk at Noelle's birthday party. He'd missed too many special occasions. He didn't want any of these wonderful days merged together in the name of expediency.

So the cake was decorated with pink roses, not red, and no Christmas wrapping paper was allowed on the table laden with gifts. The balloons were pink and yellow, and there would be no Christmas carols sung at Noelle's party.

Sixteen. He hadn't admitted it to anyone, but he was a little terrified.

He and Shock had managed to get assigned to a north Alabama task force. The assignment kept him home most of the time. When he was away for a few days, he missed his family so much it was physically painful. He had never expected to need Vic so much.

But he wasn't complaining. He was home, and he was unbearably happy.

The new house was bigger than the old one, and had a large den just perfect for entertaining. Just perfect for birthday parties. His mother was here for a few days, with Sheriff Timberlake in tow. She loved being a grandma, and she and Noelle had really hit it off. Louise was determined to spoil her granddaughter, no matter how late the date.

Wanda and her three boys were here, and so was Shock. These days, wherever Wanda was, Shock was right behind. And those kids…they adored Shock, and they listened to him, and when no one else could get the Freeman boys to behave, Shock could. The only real bump in their relationship had come when Noelle got them all to call Shock Uncle Albert. He had not been amused. Noelle had laughed for a week.

The birthday girl sidled up to him. "Can I see it again?" she whispered.

Del lifted the sleeve of his T-shirt and Noelle grinned at his new tattoo. A small ladybug with *Noelle* inscribed beneath it. He'd gotten it to celebrate not her birthday, but the fact that the papers had come through and it was official. She was now legally Noelle Wilder, a name she insisted was infinitely cooler than Noelle Lowell.

"It's smaller than Mom's," she said.

"I'm older and wiser," he said. "And it hurt."

She grinned. "You mutilated yourself for me." He knew she wanted something by the twinkle in her eye. "I'm sixteen now. Can I get a tattoo?"

"When you're thirty."

She stuck out her tongue. "According to you, I shouldn't have a *life* until I'm thirty."

"You can have a life before you turn thirty. Just no tattoo. Or drinking. Or smoking. Or—"

"Okay," she interrupted. "Jeez. Can I at least borrow the car? You are going to take me to get my license next week, right?"

"Of course. And as soon as I'm sure you're a good-enough driver, you can borrow the van."

"The van? What about the Jag?"

Del shook his head.

"I know," Noelle deadpanned. "I can borrow it when I'm thirty. You know," she said with a grin, "my thirtieth birthday is going to be *wild.*"

The doorbell rang, and Noelle and Del headed for the door at the same time. "I'll get it," Noelle said, casting him a smile. She was more beautiful than ever, her hair its natural black, the cut symmetrical, the strands softly curling around her face. "It's probably Jody."

"I don't know her."

"Him!" Noelle rolled her eyes. "My new boyfriend. Be nice!" she added.

"Where's my gun?" Del mumbled.

Noelle spun around. "Daddy!"

"I'm not going to shoot him. I just want him to know I can if it becomes necessary."

Noelle shook her head and resumed her walk to the door. "I swear, I'll be *thirty* before I get so much as a decent kiss."

"Works for me."

Noelle grunted, but she was smiling when she opened the door to a too-tall, too-cute, too-old young man. Jody had to be at least seventeen, just like the last boyfriend Del had run off.

Someone unexpected sauntered up the walk behind

Jody. The kids walked into the living room, Del giving the boy his best glare as they passed.

Instead of following his daughter and her new boyfriend inside, Del waited in the doorway.

"Wilder," Archard said crisply.

"Pops," Del said irreverently.

Archard shook his head. "I brought by some Christmas presents." He stopped there on the porch as if he intended to hand the gifts over and then leave.

"Sorry," Del said. "We're not doing Christmas today. That's tomorrow. Today is Noelle's birthday."

Archard's lips tightened. "I know that." He shifted the stack of presents, and Del saw a small box wrapped in blue. Good for the old man. "Do you think I would forget my only grandchild's birthday?"

Del leaned against the doorjamb. "She won't be the only one come next Christmas," he said.

Archard paled. "Really."

"June," he said. "The baby will be born in June."

"Congratulations," Archard said, his voice low. "If you would just…" He attempted to hand the presents over.

Del leaned forward, just slightly. "I'm going to ask you to come in and stay awhile, Pops, but I have something to say first." Vic still hadn't forgiven her father for his many transgressions. Del couldn't guarantee that she ever would. "My wife needs a father, and my daughter needs a grandfather. Up to this point, you've been pretty lousy at both jobs."

Archard's lips thinned and tightened, but he didn't argue.

"I'm giving you one more chance," he said. "If you hurt either one of them, if you insult my wife or my daughter or make them unhappy in any way, I will kick your ass out of here and you won't come back. Not ever.''

Del saw something he had not expected in the old man's eyes. Fear. Did he finally realize what he'd done? Did he have any regrets in his heart?

"Why would you give me a second chance, as you call it, after what I did to you?"

"I have a daughter now. What you did was wrong, and it ruined a good portion of my life and Vic's, but in a twisted sort of way, I understand." He thought of the skinny kid who had walked into the den with Noelle. He would do anything to protect his daughter, to keep her safe. "I understand."

Archard sniffed. "I would like to see Vic. It's been a long time."

"It won't be easy, you know," Del said. "She's pretty angry with you."

"I know."

"And you will have to attend softball games, art shows, school plays and birthday parties regularly."

Archard nodded, and Del smiled as he leaned slightly forward. "You can start by going into the den—" he pointed in the right direction "—and asking everyone what they'd like to drink. We have punch, a couple different kinds of soda and apple cider."

The old man looked taken aback, but he didn't refuse.

Del took the Christmas gifts and left Archard to carry the birthday present into the den. "My mother will show you where the kitchen is so you can get all those drinks fixed," Del called as he walked in the other direction.

He took the stairs two at a time and found Vic in the bedroom, finishing the last of her wrapping. He placed the packages in a chair by the door and walked up behind Vic to place his arms around her.

"Almost ready," she said. "I would be finished by now, but you let me nap too long."

"You need your sleep," Del said, laying his hand over her slightly rounded belly. He couldn't see the new roundness in her, not when she wore one of her flowing dresses, but he could feel it. "Everything's fine. Your father is in the kitchen, pouring drinks for everyone."

"What?" Vic turned to face him, and he tried to kiss away the horrified expression on her face.

"Everybody deserves a second chance," Del said, his mouth close to Vic's. "Even him."

Vic sighed, unconvinced but agreeable.

Downstairs, family and friends waited. Vic rested her head against his chest, closed her eyes and remained still for a long moment. He loved the way she sometimes just walked into him and stayed in this place, protected and loved and happy, at last.

"I love you," he said, smiling as he took her chin in his hand and tilted her face up so he could kiss her again.

"I love you, too." She wrapped her arms around his waist and hugged him gently.

He kissed her neck beneath her ear, where she wore two earrings. A small gold loop, and just above that, the diamond stud he had given her when he'd asked her to marry him.

It was a scary thing, to realize that without a certain person in your life you were less than you were with that person. It had been almost scary enough to send him running. Away from Vic, away from this feeling of belonging. What was worse were the moments when he stopped and wondered what his life would be like right now if he had run, if he'd never given them a chance.

Setting out to save the world was easy. Trying to save

one woman who insisted that she didn't need to be saved was the challenge of a lifetime.

Del kissed Vic's luscious neck long and slow, barely raising his lips from her flesh to speak. "Since Pops is taking care of the guests, maybe we have time for—"

"Del!" Vic interrupted, laughing.

"I can't get enough of you."

She quit laughing and held on a little tighter. "I know exactly how you feel."

"And right now, I want you all to myself." Just for a few minutes, before they went downstairs to face the mob.

It was a good day, one of the best he'd ever had. And he knew with a certainty that he'd never experienced before that their best days were ahead of them.

* * * * *

*Although you didn't meet Clint Sinclair
in this book, watch out for him when he
appears in a few months in his own story,*

CLINT'S WILD RIDE.

April will be very hot in Intimate Moments!

And don't miss

"CALLING AFTER MIDNIGHT"

*available this month in
LOVE IS MURDER,
an exciting anthology available from
Silhouette Books.*

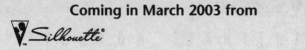
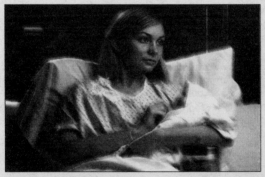

eHARLEQUIN.com

For great romance books at great prices,
shop www.eHarlequin.com today!

GREAT BOOKS:
- **Extensive selection** of today's hottest
  books, including **current** releases,
  backlist titles and new **upcoming** books.
- **Favorite authors:** Nora Roberts,
  Debbie Macomber and more!

GREAT DEALS:
- **Save every day:** enjoy great savings
  and special online promotions.
- *Exclusive* **online offers:** FREE books,
  bargain outlet savings, special deals.

EASY SHOPPING:
- Easy, secure, **24-hour shopping** from the
  comfort of your own home.
- **Excerpts, reader recommendations**
  and our **Romance Legend** will help
  you choose!
- **Convenient shipping and
  payment methods.**

**Shop online
at www.eHarlequin.com today!**

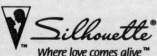

If you enjoyed what you just read,
then we've got an offer you can't resist!

Take 2 bestselling love stories FREE!

Plus get a FREE surprise gift!

Clip this page and mail it to Silhouette Reader Service™

IN U.S.A.	**IN CANADA**
3010 Walden Ave.	P.O. Box 609
P.O. Box 1867	Fort Erie, Ontario
Buffalo, N.Y. 14240-1867	L2A 5X3

YES! Please send me 2 free Silhouette Intimate Moments® novels and my free surprise gift. After receiving them, if I don't wish to receive anymore, I can return the shipping statement marked cancel. If I don't cancel, I will receive 6 brand-new novels every month, before they're available in stores! In the U.S.A., bill me at the bargain price of $3.99 plus 25¢ shipping and handling per book and applicable sales tax, if any*. In Canada, bill me at the bargain price of $4.74 plus 25¢ shipping and handling per book and applicable taxes**. That's the complete price and a savings of at least 10% off the cover prices—what a great deal! I understand that accepting the 2 free books and gift places me under no obligation ever to buy any books. I can always return a shipment and cancel at any time. Even if I never buy another book from Silhouette, the 2 free books and gift are mine to keep forever.

245 SDN DNUV
345 SDN DNUW

Name	(PLEASE PRINT)
Address	Apt.#
City	State/Prov. Zip/Postal Code

* Terms and prices subject to change without notice. Sales tax applicable in N.Y.
** Canadian residents will be charged applicable provincial taxes and GST.
  All orders subject to approval. Offer limited to one per household and not valid to current Silhouette Intimate Moments® subscribers.
  ® are registered trademarks of Harlequin Books S.A., used under license.

INMOM02   ©1998 Harlequin Enterprises Limited

Silhouette®